"Dane! There are trying to take us!

All at once Dane's body and mind synced up. No sighing. No thoughts of vacations. No molasses on the gears.

That wasn't just any woman.

It was the woman he blamed himself for making a widow.

"Rachel?"

"There are three of them! One in a van, and two—two are chasing us!"

A shout sounded in the background. Dane tightened his hold on the steering wheel, knuckles going white. The rustling noise wasn't a bad connection. It was movement. It was running.

"Rachel, where are you?"

There was more rustling and the sound of something slamming shut before she answered.

"We're at—we're at Darby Middle," she said, out of breath. "Only four of us here when they—when they showed up."

Dane cut the wheel hard, turning to the opposite direction. Another shout sounded in the background.

THE NEGOTIATION

TYLER ANNE SNELL

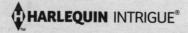
HARLEQUIN INTRIGUE®

This book is for Dianne. Not only are you the best mama-in-law I
could ask for, you're also insane. In the best way possible. Thank
you for all of your help with this series. And for creating my
favorite human. May all your days be blessed with pineapples.

ISBN-13: 978-1-335-52663-2

The Negotiation

Copyright © 2018 by Tyler Anne Snell

Recycling programs
for this product may
not exist in your area.

HARLEQUIN®
™ www.Harlequin.com

Printed in U.S.A.

Tyler Anne Snell genuinely loves all genres of the written word. However, she's realized that she loves books filled with sexual tension and mysteries a little more than the rest. Her stories have a good dose of both. Tyler lives in Alabama with her same-named husband and their mini "lions." When she isn't reading or writing, she's playing video games and working on her blog, *Almost There*. To follow her shenanigans, visit tylerannesnell.com.

Books by Tyler Anne Snell

Harlequin Intrigue

The Protectors of Riker County

Small-Town Face-Off
The Deputy's Witness
Forgotten Pieces
Loving Baby
The Deputy's Baby
The Negotiation

Orion Security

Private Bodyguard
Full Force Fatherhood
Be on the Lookout: Bodyguard
Suspicious Activities

Manhunt

Visit the Author Profile page at Harlequin.com.

CAST OF CHARACTERS

Dane Jones—This captain of the Riker County Sheriff's Department knows a thing or two about being unable to escape the pain of a mistake. Still, he's dedicated his career and life to making sure the bad guys don't win again. Even when that means sacrificing his personal life in the process. However, when the same woman he's tried to keep out of his thoughts for years calls, screaming for help, he can't turn his back on her again.

Rachel Roberts—This middle school art teacher has finally found some peace with what happened to her husband years ago. Or so she thinks. When she and one of her students are targeted, she finds herself calling on the only man other than her late husband who ever made her feel safe. With each new threat, they're forced to confront a past that nearly killed them both.

David Roberts—Rachel's late husband and Dane's best friend. His death from a hostage negotiation gone wrong shocked the sheriff's department.

Chance Montgomery—This Alabama cowboy comes into town following a clue that leads from a series of thefts in Birmingham right back to a case that's close to Dane.

Lonnie Hughes—One of Rachel's students, this twelve-year-old finds himself at the center of everyone's attention, the good guys and the bad.

Sheriff Billy Reed—Close friend and colleague to Dane, this sheriff will do everything in his power to make sure everyone within his department and county remains safe.

Saviors of the South—This group of men and women believed that the sheriff's department was corrupt and made a violent statement to prove their stance.

Prologue

Dane heard the call the same time Rachel did.

Both were sitting in the belly of the sheriff's department. They were two of several who heard what the men had to say.

"These men are sinners," the man shouted, voice slightly distorted over the speakerphone. "Plain and true! Just like this town. Just like this county. Just like this state. Sinners, all sinners!"

Dane's fists had already been balled. Now his fingers were eating into his palms. It wasn't until Rachel silently covered one hand with her own that he loosened the tension. Her wedding band was cold against his skin.

"Then why take them? They were on their way to the prison," Sheriff Rockwell said. "You're the one who kept them from facing justice."

The man on the other end of the phone call was fast to answer, like he'd rehearsed the whole thing beforehand.

"They represent corruption. A corruption that has

taken over," he said, voice still high and filled with unmistakable self-reverence. "And we, the Saviors of the South, represent the consequence to that corruption! The answer! We will show this town that this corruption will no longer be tolerated. These sinners will be the first of many demonstrations on how we will cleanse this place!"

Rachel's hand tightened over Dane's while he shared a look with the sheriff. Rockwell was a solid man who Dane had felt privileged to work alongside as his chief deputy for the past few years. He was fair, to the point and levelheaded. He was also a mean shot, and that didn't count for nothing.

"But you didn't just take prisoners," the sheriff pointed out, "you also took two guards. Two good men through and through. What's your plan with them?"

Dane held his breath. He knew Rachel was doing the same. One of those men was David Roberts. And he was one of the best of them.

That's why Rachel had married him.

That's why Dane was his best friend.

That's why both were willing to do whatever it took to get him back.

"The men who protect sinners are no better than the sinners themselves," the man answered.

Anger swelled in Dane's chest but he kept his mouth closed. Popping off at an obviously unstable man wasn't going to save David or the other guard. It wasn't going to save the inmates they had been transporting, either. Good or bad, they'd undergone trials and received a sentence by their peers. Neither Dane, the sheriff nor the Saviors of the South had any room to change those sentences. Certainly not to make the decision of whether they should live or die.

And that's really what the man on the phone was saying without saying it.

They aimed to kill the seven men they'd kidnapped that morning.

Dane knew it. The sheriff knew it. Even Rachel knew it.

She'd rushed to the department the moment she'd heard the transport van had been hit, ready to help in any way she could.

"I have money," she'd told him. "Not a lot, but maybe we can exchange it."

That had been before the call had come in. Before they'd realized the men didn't want money at all. They wanted to be heard. They wanted attention. They wanted fame.

"I can't just let you do what you want with them, no matter who they are," Sheriff Rockwell said, stern. "So let's find us a way to work this out where no one gets hurt."

The man, who would later be known as Marcus the Martyr by his followers who found themselves in prison, laughed. Without realizing it, Dane locked that sound in his memory for life. It was cold and callous. It didn't care about corruption, no matter how falsely perceived, and it didn't care about justice. It, like the man, only cared about being louder than everyone else.

Marcus wanted violence.

Dane knew it the moment he heard the man laugh and then hang up the phone.

He'd later realize it was in that moment that he knew his best friend might not make it to see the next day, but at the time all he could feel was the deep need to do something.

So when the sheriff was done cursing at the dial tone, Dane straightened and felt his world settle on his shoulders.

"I have a plan."

Chapter One

Seven years later Rachel Roberts surveyed the black-top ahead of her with a pang of annoyance. It was an early Saturday morning and the Darby Middle School building was absolutely teasing her in the background. Between her and it stood the two reasons why she was sweating in her jeans instead of lounging in her pajamas, catching up on the back-log of television shows burning a hole in her DVR.

"Now, I know none of us want to be here, but we are and that's that," she started, making sure she split her narrowed stare between both boys equally. "I guess the two of you are at that age where you don't know how ridiculous it is to call each other names in the school hallways or during class presentations, so instead of making you write long essays about compassion and being polite…"

Rachel motioned to the two buckets of chalk she'd found in the closet filled with art supplies in her classroom and the rectangle outlined in painter's tape in the middle of the blacktop. The one she'd made right before spilling her coffee onto the grass next to it. The one she'd said a few harsh words over in the silence of the school's empty front lawn.

Lonnie Hughes was the first to voice his concern. His scowl had only deepened since he'd hopped off his bike.

Lonnie was a thin twelve-year-old with tightly coiled black hair, dark, always-questioning eyes and a mouth more than ready to voice one of his many opinions. The latter was one of several reasons he was at the bottom of the school's popularity totem pole. He talked too much, listened too little and had almost no filter. This, plus an ingrained aversion to authority figures, had earned him dismissive attitudes from most of the teachers. Rachel wasn't one of them, though most of the staff had assured her that if she had more than one art class with the boy she'd think differently.

The boy standing next to him, however, was completely opposite in that respect. Teachers and students alike seemed to love Jude Carrington. Even for a seventh-grader, he had charm and was clever enough to know when to speak, what to say and how to hide all the devious things most kids that age did. His hair was a shock of red, his skin was covered in freckles, and he wore thick-framed glasses. Yet, according to Mrs. Fletcher, who had him in her homeroom, he seemed to be the leader of the seventh-grade class. Instead of being the stereotypical outcast from an '80s movie, he was Mr. Popular. With a side of bully when it came to Lonnie.

Which was why Rachel wasn't shocked to see the two of them there, though she was surprised their guardians had opted for Saturday detention instead of after school. Darby Middle rarely implemented what she called the Breakfast Club punishment. Yet here they all were.

"You want us to draw for detention?"

What I want to do is to find out what's going on with Jon Snow from Game of Thrones, she wanted to say. Instead she decided to go with a more stern response.

"Unless you really do want to write a five-page essay about why you're so sorry about what you did, I suggest you show a little enthusiasm. It wasn't exactly easy to convince Principal Martin that doing art projects was punishments for you two."

"It is when it's on a Saturday," Jude interjected.

Rachel nodded and grabbed one of the buckets.

"That's what I told him." She took out a thick piece of white chalk and sat in the middle of the empty rectangle. The blacktop was warm but nowhere near as hot as it would be by midday. If they didn't get it going now, the heat would force them inside and she'd be the one coming back in the morning to finish it alone. Rachel loved her job, but she wanted at least one day off before having to go back to it.

"This is our fall-themed mural, but I was thinking we could make it more Halloween-y. Do a bigger collage of doodles like we did in class last week to help make this slab look a bit more fun. Then, after we're done here, we're going to go inside and cut out a few hundred leaves, pumpkins and maybe some bats from construction paper. Then we're going to go hang them."

Despite his constant need to charm the adults, Jude actually groaned. Lonnie kept scowling. Rachel adopted a look caught between the two.

"Unless you want me to go inside and tell Principal Martin that you actually want to write an essay explaining why you two said what you did and how you two are going to work together in the future?" She shrugged. "I could always do this later."

For a second Rachel was afraid they would decide to go for the essays. It was fall, but in South Alabama that didn't mean much. They'd all be sweating after a few minutes. The air-conditioning inside might be enough of a draw to sway the boys from the manual labor of arts and crafts to tackling papers. Though she hoped that wasn't the case. Gaven, the principal, had mostly agreed to her suggested punishment activities because they were projects she had volunteered to do out of the goodness of her heart.

No sooner had she thought that than Rachel acknowledged it was a lie.

It hadn't just been something she'd felt she needed to do to better the school or to help raise the spir-

its of those who attended it. No. She had needed
a distraction.

One that would keep her mind away from the
one place it had been traveling recently. A place she
didn't like to visit often.

"Whatever," Lonnie finally said. Rachel breathed
an internal sigh of relief as he took a seat on the bottom line of the taped-off empty mural. Jude followed
suit but as far away from Lonnie as was possible
while staying near the chalk.

Rachel tried to clear her head as it started to fill
with sorrow. She smirked. "Glad to see we're on the
same page."

Despite Rachel's not wanting to be at school on
a Saturday, the next half hour that went by did so
with little fuss. The boys drew white, orange and
red bats and spiders and skeletons with surprising
skill. Rachel had seen both of their drawings before
in class, but there was more precision and focus in
their actions today. After Lonnie made a jab at Jude
and then Jude returned that jab before Rachel could
step in, she realized their new passion to do a good
job on the mural was probably because they were
trying to outdo each other. Meanwhile she filled the
center of the blacktop with a giant spider web. It was
oddly soothing.

"Why don't we see what Principal Martin thinks
about it before we start on the inside work?" Rachel said, stretching out her long limbs when they
were done.

Lonnie rolled his eyes.

Jude perked up. "Can I go get him?" He was already turning in the direction of the school's front doors. "Is he in his office?"

Rachel nodded but held up her index finger.

"Go straight there," she warned. Jude gave her a wide smile and was off. Lonnie looked after him, scowl back in full force.

Now it was time to try to distract someone other than herself. "I think the mural looks really good, don't you?" She pulled out her cell phone. "I'm going to take a picture. Maybe I can post it on the school's website the week of Halloween."

"Whatever," Lonnie muttered. He turned on his heel. Goodness forbid he act interested. Rachel pulled up the camera app and was readying to take the picture when he spoke up again. His tone had changed. It was like night and day. Immediately she knew something was wrong.

"Who are they?"

Rachel heard the car doors shut before she turned to see a van at the front of the parking lot a few hundred yards from them. A tall, broad-shouldered man met her stare with a smile. Sandy hair, cut short, and broad, broad shoulders. She didn't recognize him. Nor the man who had gotten out of the vehicle behind him. He wore a full set of overalls. He didn't meet her eyes.

A cold feeling of worry began to swish around in Rachel's stomach. It should have been the warning that sent her inside. However she held her spot, only instinctively taking a step forward so Lonnie was just behind her elbow. Whoever was driving the van didn't get out or cut its engine. She couldn't see the driver's face through the tint from this distance.

"Hi there," she called out to the man in front when it was clear he only had eyes for them. "Can I help you?"

The man, who she guessed was a few years older than her thirty-one, didn't lessen his stride over the curb and onto the grass. He was coming straight for them, his friend at his back.

"Yes, ma'am, you can," he answered, voice carrying through the air with ease. "I'm looking for someone." His eyes moved to Lonnie for the briefest of moments. "Maybe you two can help me out."

That cold in Rachel's stomach began to expand to the rest of her. She tightened her grip on the phone. Her gut with it.

"Maybe you'd like to talk to the people inside," she responded. Her voice had climbed to an octave that would let anyone who knew her well enough realize something was off. She was trying to tamp down the growing sense of vulnerability, even around her lie. "They'd probably know better than anyone who's around. We've been outside all morning."

The only people inside the school were Gaven and Jude, but at the moment, all Rachel wanted to do was to curb the men's attention. Darby Middle was nestled between one of the small town's main roads, a wide stretch of trees that hid an outlet of houses and an open field for sale that had once been used for farming. This being Saturday morning or not, there were rarely people out and about who could see the front lawn of the school. The two men continuing, unperturbed, was a reminder of just how quiet the world around them was.

Who were the men?

Why were they at a middle school on a Saturday morning?

Was she overreacting?

Sandy Hair's smile twisted into a grin. Like she'd just told a joke that only he knew the punch line to. He kept an even pace but was getting close enough to make her stomach knot.

Something isn't right.

The thought pulsed through her mind so quickly that it physically moved her another step over. This time cutting Lonnie off from the men's view altogether.

"Nah," Sandy Hair answered. "I think you will do just fine."

In that moment Rachel knew two things.

One, something was about to happen and it wasn't going to be good. She wasn't a pro at reading people, but there were some nuances that were easy to pick up. The way the man in the overalls looked between her and Lonnie and then back to the building behind them. The way he tilted his body ever so slightly forward as if he was getting ready to move. The way his partner's eyes narrowed and his nostrils flared. The men were about to do something.

Which was how, two, she knew her gut had been right to worry. She should have listened sooner. While there was an unwritten law of Southern hospitality her parents had taught her from the moment she could walk and talk, Rachel wasn't about to give the men the benefit of the doubt. Not any longer. She'd learned the hard way that there were bad people in the world who did bad things.

They'd taken David from her.

She wasn't going to let another set of them take her or the child at her side.

And with a shock of adrenaline, Rachel realized that was what they were about to try to do.

There was about to be running.

There was about to be chasing.

So Rachel decided she wanted her and Lonnie to have the head start. Holding on to her cell phone like the lifeline it might become, Rachel spun on her heel and grabbed Lonnie's hand. "Run!"

Chapter Two

Dane Jones, for once, wasn't in the office. Instead he was at the park, sitting on a bench with Chance Montgomery, trying to convince the man that there wasn't a conspiracy about to swallow Riker County whole.

"It's been a helluva year—I'll be the first to admit that," Dane said. "But it sure does feel like you're looking for trouble that's not there. And we surely don't need any more trouble here."

Chance, formerly a private investigator from around Huntsville, Alabama, was what Dane liked to call a pot-stirrer, among other things. He was a good man and had been a good friend over the years, but he had the nasty habit of not just getting antsy when he was bored but turning into somewhat of a lone ranger detective when the mood struck him. It occasionally reminded Dane how different he was from the man.

Dane was contemplative. The kind of man who worked well in the quiet. Chance was brash. He spoke up, out, and didn't think twice about the feathers he ruffled, especially when he was between jobs as he was now.

"I'm telling you, Dane, something isn't adding up around here," he implored. "Last week three warehouses were unloaded in Birmingham. All weird stuff, too. Radio equipment, dog crates and enough bubble wrap to wrap an eighteen-wheeler were stolen at the same time."

"I'm not saying that isn't strange," Dane admitted. "I just don't see why you've come to me with the information. We're several hours away from Birmingham. I can't see how I could help from here. Or why it would fall into my purview at all."

Chance took off his cowboy hat and put it on his knee. He came from a long line of Alabama cowboys. They didn't just wear the hats or have the accents, they had the attitude of an old Western movie lead. Dane wouldn't even be surprised if Chance practiced drawing his pistols back at his family farmland outside the county. The same land Chance retreated to when he had nothing else to do. Or, again, got bored. Like he must have been now if he was looking into thefts of mass amounts of bubble wrap.

"I'm telling you because one of the vans spotted loading up the crates had a plate that traced back to a deceased Bates Hill resident."

That caught Dane's attention. Bates Hill was the smallest town in Riker County, which put it square in the sheriff's department jurisdiction. It also made

Chance's insistence that they meet make more sense. Still, he wasn't about to jump to any conclusions.

"Who did it trace back to?"

Chance dug into his jeans' pocket and pulled out a piece of paper. He handed it over but read the name out loud.

"Tracy Markinson," he said. "Ring a bell?"

Dane felt like he'd jammed both feet in a bucket of ice water. His mind skidded to a halt and instead of staying in the present where it was needed, it did one hell of a job throwing itself backward.

"Rings a loud one." Dane looked at the paper but only saw the face of a man he'd never forget. "Tracy Markinson's been dead for almost a decade," he said. "Definitely not stealing bubble wrap in Birmingham."

Chance slid his finger around the brim of his hat and then thumped it once. "Which is why I thought I needed to take a drive out to see you." He cast Dane a knowing look. "And why I thought talking in private might be the best move. I didn't want to waltz into the department and just throw this at you. Thought doing it here, in the fresh air, might be better. Plus, you know how much I hate offices."

Dane didn't speak for a moment. He was seeing ghosts. Ghosts of his past. Ghosts he'd created. And where there were ghosts, there was her.

He didn't say it, but Dane was glad Chance had told him outside the department. He prided himself on being surefooted when it came to his job. Right now? Right now he felt like he was treading air.

"How exactly did it trace back to him?" he finally asked. Even to his ears his voice had gone low, nearing a whisper. "You said license plate?"

"Yes, sir. It was attached to a burgundy van that left the warehouse with the dog crates. Tracy was the last person who legally owned it, but past that, I'm not sure on any more details. Once I saw the name, I thought I'd come talk to you first."

Dane's gears were still moving slow. Like a cup of molasses had been poured over them. He'd worked a lot of cases since Tracy was killed. Ones that had made his blood boil. Ones that had kept him up at night. Ones that had shaken the entire sheriff's department and county to their cores. Yet what had happened to Tracy? That was a case that had changed Dane's entire life in the blink of an eye.

An eye that might be looking at him now.

"After Tracy died, his things were given to the family he had left and then the rest were donated, if I'm not mistaken. Birmingham might be far for some, but it's definitely within driving distance. Not hard to get his van up there. It could be just a coincidence that it happened to be his old one," Dane pointed out.

Chance picked his cowboy hat off his leg and put it on. He looked out at the small park and the autumn leaves that had started to fall. The scene contrasted with the heat that hadn't yet left South Alabama.

"It could be," he admitted. "Coincidence, maybe. Bad luck, maybe that, too. But my gut says it's not, and I aim to find out why it's telling me that." Chance stood. "I'll be at the hotel on Cherry for a few days, looking into some things. You've got my number. Don't hesitate to call it. I'll do the same if I find anything. Unless you want me to keep this one out of your hair?"

Dane shook his head.

"If there is a loop, keep me in it if you don't mind," Dane said. "And, Chance? Thanks for reaching out."

The cowboy gave a small nod and walked over the fallen leaves to his truck in the parking lot. Dane watched as he drove away. Riker County was nothing short of surprising, no matter the season. It might only house one large city, but the trouble that found its way into its borders never ceased to amaze Dane. If it wasn't a new criminal organization trying to take over, it was kidnapped children, manhunts and enough gunshots traded between the bad guys and their department to last him a few lifetimes.

Dane left the bench in an attempt to exit his current road of thought.

Even before the recent uptick in chaos around his home, there had been only one night that had burned its way into his soul.

The night he'd made a decision.

The wrong one.

Dane hopped into his truck and pointed it toward the department in the heart of Carpenter, Alabama.

He had too much on his plate to fight with his past again. Now wasn't the time.

He turned the volume up on the radio, let a crooning song croon, and was about to write off Chance's gut when his phone vibrated in his pocket.

"I need a vacation," he told the cab of his truck, fishing out the ringing phone. "One where I just don't answer this blasted phone." Hell, he'd needed one for years now. No time like the present, right?

Dane didn't recognize the number but unlocked his phone all the same. As the captain of the Investigative Bureau at the Riker County's Sheriff's Department, he had to be always ready for the unknown. Not to ignore it just because it was easy. Life wasn't easy. There was no reason to suspect work would be, either.

He turned down the radio and cleared his throat. "Captain Jones, here."

"Dane!" The sound of a bad connection was almost as loud as the woman's scream. On reflex he held the phone away from his ear for a moment. "Dane! There are men at the school trying to take us!"

All at once Dane's body and mind synced. No sighing. No thoughts of vacations. No molasses on the gears.

That wasn't just any woman.

It was the widow he'd helped make seven years ago.

"Rachel?"

"There are three of them! One in a van and two—two are chasing us!"

A shout sounded in the background. Dane tightened his hold on the steering wheel, knuckles going white. The rustling noise wasn't a bad connection. It was movement. It was running.

"Rachel, where are you?"

There was more rustling and the sound of something slamming shut before she answered.

"We're in—we're inside Darby Middle," she said, out of breath. "Only four of us here when they—when they showed up."

Dane cut the wheel hard, turning in the opposite direction. Another shout sounded in the background.

This time the shout was closer.

"We gotta hide," came a small voice, much closer to the phone. A student at school on a Saturday? Rachel didn't get a chance to respond before someone else was yelling.

"Rach—" Dane started. She cut him off.

"Dane, there're children here," she stressed. Something made a scrapping noise.

The fear in her voice was unmistakably true and poignant. It stirred something inside Dane's chest he didn't have time to investigate.

"Dane, please hurry!"

Dane pressed his gas pedal to the floor. Any more force and it felt like it would have gone through the floorboard.

"I'm coming," he promised, voice rising to show he meant it. "Just stay on the—"

A series of crashes cut him off again. There was another wave of rustling. This time it sounded violent.

On cue Rachel cried out.

"Rachel," Dane yelled into the receiver.

"Ms. Roberts!"

"Run, Lonnie," she yelled in response. But it wasn't to him. Instead Dane felt like he was under water, unable to break the surface to get to her.

"Run!"

Dane heard a new voice. It belonged to a man. An angry one at that.

"Oh no, you don't," he yelled.

Dane held the phone away from his ear again as a loud crash reverberated out of it. "Rachel!"

But it was too late. The call dropped.

And then Dane was left alone with nothing but silence.

THE FINGERS THAT threaded into her long hair were angry. They wasted little time in pulling her backward in one violent motion. The change in Rachel's momentum was jarring. She yelled out as she fell into the man in overalls, feet coming out from under her.

There was a moment of pause when her terrified mind let her know that she could give up right then. It would be easier to let the men take her, especially since one had her by the hair. Like trying to hold your breath under water as long as you could but having to surface and breathe in air when you couldn't stay down any longer.

"Rachel!"

Dane's voice coming through her dropped phone was small compared to that of the man at her back, but it heralded in her good sense. She wasn't going to let terror seize her body; she wasn't going to let the men, either. With both hands, she did something David had once showed her. Cupping both hands, she threw them up and behind her with all the force she could muster at this awkward angle. Her head burned where he was pulling her hair, but her hands slapped over the man's ears with surprising precision.

He howled in response. The pain at her roots lessened as he let go.

However he wasn't the only man in the room. No sooner had she scrambled to her feet than the sandy-haired man lunged at her. Rachel didn't have time to ready to fend him off. Luckily she didn't have to. A large-bristled broom swung so close to her head she felt the wind off it seconds before it connected with her attacker's face. Instead of swinging it around again, the broom's wielder used it like a batting ram, charging forward enough that it sent the surprised man on his backside.

Lonnie let get of the handle when she was clear. Rachel didn't have time to thank the boy for saving her. The men behind her were a tangle of limbs but neither was hurt enough to be down for too long. She and Lonnie had to get away.

She grabbed his hand again and ran toward the second doorway leading out of the classroom. While she was seeking safety, Rachel had run in the opposite direction of the front office. She didn't know where Jude was and didn't want to chance having him walk out in the middle of the men.

"You bitch," one of the men yelled from the other room. The sound of desks overturning followed. Rachel tightened her grip on Lonnie's arm and skidded around the hallway corner. They'd been lucky that the study hall room had been open. The rest of the classrooms were not. If she'd needed any open for decorating, she was supposed to go to Gaven to unlock them.

Now?

Now she was doing the fastest recall she'd ever attempted, trying to remember which doors might be open while adrenaline had her heart thumping a mile a minute, trying to drill itself out of her chest.

Heavy footsteps echoed down the hallway they'd just left.

Rachel didn't want to admit it, but they were running out of time and out of distance.

She just hoped they weren't also running out of luck.

Chapter Three

The heat from outside did nothing to break through the chill that had fallen in the cab of his truck. It moved into Dane's bones and stayed there even when he screeched to a stop in front of Darby Middle and jumped out onto the lawn.

In the time it had taken to book it over to the school, he'd called everyone on the horn that could help. Local PD had a cruiser on the way. Billy was sending deputies and flooring it over, too, and their dispatcher, Cassie, had even managed to contact the principal. Gaven Martin had been given orders to protect himself and one of the children who had been at the school. He'd also confirmed that the only other people at Darby Middle were Rachel and another student named Lonnie.

It was nice to have so much communication and movement on the ground. However the time it took to get from point A to B had stretched too long. Dane's gut dropped to his feet when he saw the parking lot was empty. No driver. No van.

Which meant the mystery men, or at least one of them, had left the premises.

Dane only hoped Rachel and the boy hadn't been along for the ride.

He pulled his gun out and didn't stop long enough to even think about waiting for backup. Instead he hurried to the front double doors like the devil himself was nipping at his heels.

Dane didn't have any kids, and the ones he did occasionally babysit for friends didn't live in Darby. Point of fact, he'd never been inside the middle school before. A wave of cool air mixed with the faint smell of cleaning supplies pressed against his face as he moved from the outside concrete to the beige tile inside. The door shutting behind him was the only sound that reverberated across the hall in front of him. For once, the quiet didn't sit right with him.

He held his gun higher and went to the glass door closest to him marked Main Office. It was locked. Another closed door could be seen at the end of the room with the principal's nameplate across it. Gaven and the other student were hiding on the other side.

Dane moved his attention back to the hallway in front of him. It cut to the right and was empty. Closed doors lined each side along with small lockers around the bottom half of the walls. Dane stayed alert as he hurried to the first set of doors. Both were locked. He went to the next two. They were also locked. He kept on until there was a room with a door wide open. His heart hammered in his chest. Some of the desks inside had been toppled over, a broomstick was broken in two and, in the middle of it all, there was a discarded cell phone.

Dane didn't bother picking it up. He knew it belonged to Rachel.

This was where she must have fought the men.

Her cry echoed in Dane's mind.

He hadn't liked hearing it over the phone.

He didn't like remembering, either.

Moving as quietly as he could, Dane exited the room through its second door. If Rachel had run in through the main school entrance and then into the classroom, he'd bet she would have gone deeper into the school rather than back outside. That was *if* she had broken away from the men and wasn't in their custody now.

Dane shook his head.

He wasn't going to think about that just yet.

The adjoining hallway led to another that formed three sides of a box that made up the school. Most of the doors were shut and locked. Dane checked the bathrooms quickly and wordlessly. Nothing seemed out of the ordinary. No one made a sound. If Rachel and Lonnie had run this way, their options to hide had been limited. By the time he made it to the end of another hallway, he worried that they might not have had the chance to even make it that far.

But then he saw it. An open door at the end of the hall.

Dane hurried over. The door led into a small

gym. Bleachers were pulled out, a few soft mats were pushed into the corner and light from outside streamed in through the tall windows on either side of the room. Two doors that must have led to the locker rooms were located on the far wall, another was in the corner and had a set of locked chains around the handles. A soccer field, surrounded by trees, at the end of the property could be seen through the glass on the top half of each door.

Or at least where the glass had been.

One window was completely busted out.

Dane cursed beneath his breath as he got closer. There was blood on the broken glass. Someone had busted it in an attempt to escape. Dane cursed again as he shook the handle of one of the doors. The chains clinked their objections. If Rachel had broken out of the school, she must have been desperate.

Dane lowered his gun and kicked the door hard.

He should have been there sooner.

He should have—

Movement out of the corner of his eye made him spin on his heel. His gun came up high and ready.

"Dane?"

Rachel peeked out from under the closest set of bleachers. A boy was at her side.

Dane could have sung in relief.

While it had been years since he'd seen the woman in person, he realized right then and there he hadn't forgotten the details of what made Rachel Rachel.

Her hair might be shorter, but it was still dark,

smooth and straight. It framed a long, thin face with high cheekbones and a faint dimple in her chin. Her complexion was tanned, though, if memory served him correctly, Dane would bet it was a farmer's tan. Rachel had always liked to go outside but wasn't a fan of sunbathing. He'd often teased her when she wore shorts and her ankles and feet were different shades.

But of all the details Dane remembered, it was her eyes that made him feel like they were suddenly in the past.

Denim blue. Like a favorite pair of worn blue jeans.

They fastened to him now, a mix of emotions he didn't have time to separate and examine. "Are you two okay?"

He lowered his gun but didn't holster it. Just because he hadn't seen the mystery men didn't mean he was letting down his guard.

"Yeah, we're—" Rachel started but the boy, Lonnie, interrupted.

"She cut herself good when she broke the window," he said, voice stronger than Dane would expect in the situation. He motioned to her arm. It was pressed against her chest, her other hand cradling her wrist.

"It's not that bad. Just a little blood. I'm fine." She must have read the question in his expression. "I thought if it looked like we made it outside, *they* would go outside and we could hide and wait it out here."

Dane couldn't deny that plan was impressive, if not risky. "The van you said was out front is gone. And, as far as I could tell, the rest of the school is empty. Except for Gaven and the other student."

Rachel had opened her mouth, worry already in her eyes, when he hurried to add, "Who are both fine and locked in the office."

Rachel let out a sigh of relief, but her body didn't start to relax until a welcomed sound started in the distance.

Sirens.

Dane flashed the boy a small smile. "Backup has arrived."

THE EMT HAD cleaned and bandaged the cut along the top of her wrist but hadn't gotten to scolding her until he'd looked at the swollen parts of her knuckle.

"You're lucky the glass was already compromised," he had said. "Or else you might have *broken* your hand instead. It's going to hurt for a few days, regardless."

Rachel had kept her mouth shut on the EMT's commentary. While he had only been trying to help, he hadn't been the one running through the school trying to keep away from men hell-bent on grabbing her and the kid in her care. She had broken the window because she *was* going to try to get Lonnie and herself through. They'd already used up their luck by losing the two men for a minute or two, giving them enough time to get into the gym. But the moment after she'd cleared the glass away, Rachel had made a split-second decision to keep hiding.

Guilt and worry and fear wound around her stomach, even though she was now safe. It was just dumb luck that the men had seen the broken window and believed what she had wanted them to. That she had run to the woods with Lonnie at her side. Once they'd seen the empty window, they'd run in the opposite direction, both swearing.

It could easily have gone the other way.

Now Rachel was sitting in the Riker County Sheriff's Department, staring at a nameplate that read Captain Dane Jones and struggling to shake loose the added sorrow trying to creep in. Even without the morning she'd just had, being in the building was enough to turn her mood. Down the hall, years ago, she'd listened to Dane and his colleagues attempt to do their best to save her husband.

She'd seen the way their bodies had been as tense as hers as they'd gone through each scenario with vigor. The way their determination had kept their brows furrowed and their lips thinned. The way they'd tried to assure her everything would be okay.

However, perhaps the singular thing she remembered most from that day was just after the storm had broken outside and Dane had walked in. She'd been waiting for news, but the department had gone radio silent. Though, she realized later, the silence was for her. They were just waiting for Dane to come back. Waiting for him to tell her.

And there he had been, walking through the hallway with rain clinging to his clothes and sliding off his hair. He wasn't walking with purpose. He'd been walking on reflex.

Rachel fisted her hand in her lap.

She had known the moment their eyes had met that David was gone.

That day had put a hole in her heart, one that had only grown as the year went on.

Now?

She looked down at the bandage on her arm and felt the dull ache of her swollen hand.

Now, after more time had passed, it was less of a hole and more like a window. She could see the memories in the distance and occasionally, if she opened the window, she could feel their joy and sorrow they often brought.

Rachel smiled to herself with no real mirth.

She'd been a widow for years and yet always around the anniversary of David's death she found herself revisiting the day when the word was still so foreign. After the day she'd had, though, she supposed she shouldn't be too harsh on herself.

The door behind her opened and Dane pushed through. He didn't look at her as he put a file on his desk, along with his phone, and then settled into his chair. This had been par for the course between them after she gave her statement. He'd been avoiding her.

Just as he'd been doing for years.

An old anger started to weave itself around her chest again, making her hot.

She cleared her voice.

"Any luck finding the men?" she started, hopeful.

Dane was already shaking his head before she finished.

"No one has been able to pin down the men or their vehicle, but there's an all-points bulletin out." He met her gaze. His eyes were hard, dark. "We're running your and Lonnie's descriptions of the men through our database, seeing if anyone matches. Hopefully we'll get a hit so we can make some moves."

"And if they aren't in the database?"

Dane's expression softened, if only a little. "Don't worry, we'll find them. It's not a matter of if, just a matter of when." On cue, a knock sounded against the doorway. A man with a detective's shield around his neck gave her a curt nod.

"Rachel, this is one of our newest detectives, Caleb Foster. You might remember Detective Matt Walker, but currently he's enjoying his honeymoon." Dane's tone changed, if only briefly, to humor. "But it pains me to admit this, Foster here is more than capable of getting to the bottom of this."

This time the detective chuckled. He extended his hand, which Rachel took with a smile.

"If Dane has faith in you, you must have deserved

it," she responded truthfully. The detective nodded and then all humor was gone.

"The chief is here and wants to talk to us ASAP. I tried to tell him you were busy, but—"

"But the anxious chief of Darby PD waits for no woman or man when he's ready to get some answers," Dane finished.

The detective nodded.

"All right, tell him I'm coming."

Caleb said a quick goodbye to her and was gone as fast as it took Dane to get out of his chair. His brow was furrowed. He was already miles away from her.

And that brought the anger back.

"I'm going home," she said before he could disappear on her again. "Unless there's something else I need to do? Or there's something else you need to say?"

Dane paused midstep. For a moment Rachel thought he was going to actually talk to her about something, but he did what the Dane from the past few years had done perfectly.

He took the easy way out and avoided her.

"No, that's all," he said. "We'll call you if we have any more questions or need to follow up."

"And how do I get back to my car?" she pressed.

"I'll send someone in to take you back."

Rachel knew her expression had hardened. She felt the anger tensing her up. Dane started to say something more but hesitated. She remembered a time when they'd had no problem talking.

But now everything was different.

"I'm glad you're okay," he finally said, though his eyes were already on the door.

Rachel waited until he was gone to respond. "Thanks for picking up the phone."

Chapter Four

Dane was a jackass, plain and true. He thought it the moment he left his office and he thought it through his meeting with Darby's chief of police, Detective Foster, and Riker County's sheriff, Billy Reed. A meeting that had gone over their limited facts and debated who would handle the case, seeing as it had happened outside the sheriff's department's jurisdiction.

However, unlike Dane, Billy was a charmer. The people of Riker County loved their sheriff, and that included the chiefs of police from the towns and city that they encompassed. When Billy took office, he had worked hard to keep relations between all local law enforcement friendly, so when the time arose where they wanted to cash in some favors, it wasn't frowned upon. At least, not for long.

Dane grabbed a water from the break room afterwards and sat down at one of the tables, relieved the chief had agreed to let them take lead. He wondered if he would have been able to talk the man into it had he followed through and become sheriff when he'd had the opportunity. He had a familiar pang of regret at the question. He remembered his younger self, eyes wide and mind set on leading the sheriff's department when Sheriff Rockwell had been around.

But things had changed.

Now he was just the jackass who had gotten their off-duty dispatcher to take Rachel back to the school instead of doing it himself.

After all she had been through, there he was, still trying to put distance between them.

Guilt, old and new, created tension in his shoulders. Dane rolled them back. It didn't help.

"So there I was, coming out of my doctor's appointment, when I run into a very peculiar scene." Dane turned to see the sheriff's right-hand woman, Chief Deputy Suzy Simmons-Callahan, in the doorway of the break room, brow raised and hand on her pregnant belly. Even with a rounded stomach, Suzy was not to be taken lightly. "Chance Montgomery and that black cowboy hat of his asking the vet next door about dog crates and bubble wrap. Know anything about that? Because I can't imagine that man being in town and not dropping by to see you."

Dane nodded. "We met this morning. He's following a case in Birmingham involving a series of thefts."

"Dog crates and bubble wrap?"

"And radio equipment."

Suzy sat down at his table, curiosity clear in her

eyes. "And why is he here? We might occasionally work with other counties, but usually that county is next to us, not hours away."

Dane sighed. He had planned on keeping what Chance had told him under his hat, but he wasn't about to lie to Suzy. She was one of the few friends he'd kept throughout the past few years. He'd like to keep it that way for many more.

"A vehicle at one of the crime scenes was registered to Tracy Markinson." Suzy looked down at her hands, brow pulling in.

He gave her a second to remember. Then it was written all over her face.

"It definitely wasn't Markinson driving, if that's what Chance was after," she said.

Dane nodded. "That's why he's in Riker County. He's following the vehicle's trail."

"And asking local vets about dog crates and bubble wrap," she added with a grin.

"I never claimed to know his methods." He mimicked the grin. "He told me he'd keep me in the loop if he did find anything, but I'm sure I'll see him sooner rather than later, especially after what happened earlier."

They both sobered.

"I'm glad Rachel and the boy were okay," she said. "But I'll tell you what I told Billy, it sure doesn't make sense what happened. Though I guess a lot of the things we deal with don't make sense to us. Some people just do what they want, and sometimes what they want makes my blood boil."

"You've got that right."

He didn't need to ask Suzy to clarify her viewpoint. It *didn't* make sense that Rachel and Lonnie had been targeted. Even if it had been a crime of opportunity, abducting two people in broad daylight in a public place was brave.

And stupid.

The worst kind of combination when it came to the criminal mind.

"And how are you doing?" she asked. It was Dane's turn to raise his eyebrow. She clarified. "Not one but two reminders of the past all within one morning? That has to be *interesting* for you."

"It definitely wasn't how I thought today would go," he admitted, hedging on a concrete answer. "But I guess part of living in and around small towns means that eventually we all run into our pasts. One way or the other."

Suzy surprised him with a laugh. "If I was Deputy Ward I'd tell you that you sound like a fortune cookie." She got up and patted her stomach with another laugh.

"Good thing you aren't Deputy Ward," he deadpanned.

Suzy waved him off. "You did good today, Captain. Just make sure you don't stay here all night. Like your cowboy friend said, we'll keep you in the loop if anything happens. Until then let's trust our women and men out in the field."

"Sure thing, Suzy."

Dane watched her disappear into the hallway and finished off his water. She *was* right. It had been years since the Saviors of the South had terrorized the department. In the time after, he'd managed to limit how much exposure he had to reminders of that fateful day. Even when it had been hard.

His thoughts went back to a pair of blue eyes.

Angry blue eyes.

Dane pulled out his phone. He went to Recent Calls.

Who were the men who had gone after Rachel? And why?

HER NEIGHBOR MARNIE GABLE was front and center the moment Rachel drove up to her house later that night. No sooner had her door opened than she was enveloped in a tight, teary embrace. Marnie's wild hair of curls even seemed to be trying to pull her in.

"You could have died," she squalled.

Rachel rubbed her back and smiled. "But I didn't."

Marnie pulled back so Rachel could see the shine in her eyes but didn't let go. "But—"

"But I didn't," Rachel interrupted. "I'm here and okay."

Marnie was a ball of energy at any given time, but as Rachel gently pulled away from her, she saw that the girl was barely holding it together. She had really been scared.

Rachel felt a tug at her heartstrings.

Marnie wasn't just a neighbor, she was the daughter of her neighbor. Rachel had somewhat adopted the young woman, just twenty-one now, as a friend when she was a teen. Her parents often traveled for work and Rachel had been the ideal babysitter, if only for location. Both of their houses were out in the most rural part of Darby. It was a fair drive from town no matter where you were coming from. There was even a good distance between their two houses. Marnie used to ride her bike over. Now she drove her beat-up green Beetle.

Marnie didn't seem to believe her claims of being okay. She detached herself and moved to the side so the security light could help her see Rachel better. Her eyes widened when they took in her bandaged wrist and bruised knuckles.

Rachel beat her to addressing them.

"Just some minor aches and pains," she hurried to explain. "Nothing too bad." Rachel tried on a reassuring smile and walked around the woman to the front porch. She pulled out her keys.

"I just don't get it," Marnie said, following. "Who were those creeps? What were they doing?"

A burst of cool air pushed against them as they moved into the house. Rachel felt tension she didn't realize she'd been holding start to seep out. From the back of the house a string of meows started.

"That's the mystery of it all," Rachel responded. She made a beeline for the kitchen at the side of the house. The sliding-glass door that lined one wall showed the soft glow of the garden lights she'd set up along the side deck. It was comforting in a way. "It's still an open investigation."

June the Cat's meows got louder. Rachel pulled her dry food from the pantry and headed for her bowl. She paused before pouring. "Wait, how did you hear about what happened?"

Marnie managed to look sheepish. "I heard about it on the radio, or at least, they said something had happened at the school. After that I kind of went into snooping mode. Called a few people until I found someone who knew something."

Rachel gave her a stern glance. "What have I told you about looking into the gossip mill?"

Marnie huffed but answered.

"That the answers aren't worth the trouble," she said. "And just looking for those answers usually only makes more gossip for others."

Rachel nodded. June the Cat looked up at her with mild interest.

"Well, I was worried," Marnie grumbled. "So sue me." She went to the breakfast bar and plopped down. Rachel took advantage of the silence to reheat some leftover lasagna. She cut an extra piece and slid it to her guest. It was enough to get the young woman talking again.

"I just can't believe it happened is all," she said around a bite. "And they haven't even caught the men? I mean, what if they didn't just try to grab you because you were out in the open? What if it's *you* they wanted to begin with?"

Rachel was already gearing up to combat Marnie's worries but came up short. Not because what Marnie had said made sense—she'd already entertained the thought, though she'd pushed it away just as quickly—but because light moved across the deck.

Headlights.

"Your mom wasn't coming over tonight, was she?" Rachel asked, hopeful.

Marnie put her fork down. She shook her head.

"She's in Tennessee for the week." Rachel pulled out her phone.

"Great," she muttered. It was dead. The battery rarely lasted an entire day without needing a charge. She'd been meaning to get a new one for months.

Marnie peeked over her shoulder. "Are *you* expecting anyone?"

"No, but I also wasn't expecting you." Rachel gave her a quick smile but it didn't stay long. She left her plate and hurried into the bedroom and straight to her closet. She bent in front of the safe David had insisted they have and typed in the combo. When Rachel turned around holding a handgun, Marnie was there to gasp.

"Stay here," Rachel warned.

Marnie's eyes were the size of quarters but she listened.

Rachel went into the hallway, slowly moving across the hardwood to the front of the house. Her earlier insistence that she was okay started to fade away. The weight of the gun in her bandaged hand helped remind her that things could have turned out a lot differently this morning. And they still could. Every step she took toward the front door ate up her calm.

Was she overreacting?

Had she just been in the wrong place at the wrong time at the school?

Or were the men coming for *her*?

She tightened her grip on the gun. Her nerves shook her hand. The muscles in her legs readied to run. It didn't help matters when a booming knock sounded against the front door.

She paused, a few feet from it.

There were no windows to show her who it was, so she walked softly to the peephole. Holding her breath, heart in her throat, Rachel looked through it.

"Holy buckets." She breathed out and lowered the gun to her side. She opened the door in time to catch Dane's fist in midair. He was quick to take in her expression and the weapon.

"Before you use that on me, know that, in my defense, I called you. Three times, in fact."

It wasn't lost on Rachel how much seeing the man

made her feel better. Just as seeing him standing in the gym, cursing at the chained doors, had this morning. Capable, sturdy, a force to be reckoned with. Handsome, too. Though that wasn't anything new.

"I just realized my phone died," she said, trying to get her heartbeat back on its normal path.

Dane motioned to the gun. "Well, I'm glad to see that you're more cautious than not. It makes my—the department's—job easier in making sure you stay safe." His eyes strayed over her shoulder as footsteps echoed up the hallway.

"Everything okay?" Marnie called out.

Rachel turned to find the woman holding something in her hands. It surprised a laugh out of her. "Yeah, Marnie. Everything is fine, but is that my bedside lamp?"

Marnie shrugged.

"I wanted to help," she said defensively. She raised her chin a fraction, proud.

"Well, you can help by putting that back. Please."

Marnie rolled her eyes but went back into the bedroom.

Dane grinned.

"I guess it's a good thing I didn't just barge in," he said. "If a bullet didn't do me in, the lamp just might have."

A look she couldn't place passed over Dane's expression. He took a small step backward and jutted his thumb over his shoulder. His truck was parked at the mouth of the drive, since there was no true curb around the property unless you drove back to the two-lane that connected to the town. "Everyone's still looking for the men, but until we have more information, I thought I might hang out here for a while, just as a precaution."

Rachel couldn't stop her surprise from surfacing.

"Deputy Ward is keeping an eye out on Lonnie, too," he added.

She recovered. "Oh, yeah. Well, that's good. Especially after everything Lonnie went through today. Better safe than sorry."

Rachel omitted that she felt another surge of relief having someone so close. It was only after he started to turn away that she wondered if that feeling was because her someone just happened to be Dane.

"Okay, well, charge your cell and give me a heads-up if anyone else is coming over," he said, already moving down the steps. "I'll see you in the morning."

"Hey, Dane."

The words left Rachel's mouth before her mind could catch them. Dane turned, but his expression was blank. He was shutting down.

Again.

Still, Rachel was riding the high of feeling relief and, after the day she'd had, she didn't want it to stop.

"You could stay inside," she said. "In the spare room or on the couch. It isn't like you haven't slept on either before."

She tried to smile. She really did. She tried to remember the man who had been her husband's best friend. The man who had been *her* friend. The one who had smiled and joked and never turned down an invitation from them to come over.

But time had a funny way of making memories hurt, even when they were good ones.

And maybe that showed.

Dane shook his head and averted his gaze. "I can't."

He went back to his truck without another word.

Then, all at once, Rachel felt her anger returning.

This time it was aimed at a man named Marcus. Not only had he taken her husband from her, he'd all but taken her friend, too.

Chapter Five

Rachel took her coffee out onto the back patio the next morning. It was her second cup and not strong enough to combat her nearly sleepless night. Every time she seemed to close her eyes, there was the sandy-haired man smiling at her. Then there was Overalls grabbing her hair. Both images together and separate had gotten her out of bed and roaming the house. Or, really, going to the front windows and peeking out to see if Dane's truck was still there.

It had been.

Every single time.

Now she was trying not to think too much and just hoping the caffeine would kick in and make her feel less sluggish. And more normal.

The sun shone through the tops of the pine trees and warmed the wooden rail she was leaning against. The side patio would always be her favorite spot in the world, she was sure. Worn, in need of a new coat of stain, and filled with past moments when she'd spent countless hours across its surface, it was Rachel's idea of peaceful.

She looked out toward the creek in the distance. It wound around the two acres of her land in a half circle before going through the next two properties. She remembered how much she'd disliked having water near the house when she'd moved into David's family home right after they married, perpetually afraid of flooding that never came. Now it was her favorite feature. She supposed there was some comfort in the fact that no matter how unexpected the turns her life took, she could look out at that creek and watch it keep going the same way it had been going for years.

It didn't stop for tragedy.

It didn't stop for sorrow.

It didn't stop just because there were bad men with bad intentions out there.

It just kept going.

Rachel sighed into her coffee.

Clearing her head wasn't as easy as she'd hoped.

Her thoughts turned to Lonnie. If she was having a hard time coping with what had happened, then she had to believe Lonnie might be struggling, too. Playing it tough in the schoolyard or in the hallways was one thing. He might have held it together at the school and in the department before his uncle had picked him up, but now that it had had time to settle?

Rachel tightened her grip around the coffee cup.

She kept her gaze on the creek. There it was, apathetic to how rapidly her thoughts jumped from fear to worry and then to anger.

Yesterday had felt like one long dance between her and Dane, both trying to move around each other without getting too close. She knew why she'd done it. Anger and frustration. But him? He'd pawned her off on a stranger once she needed to leave the department. The old Dane? Her friend? He wouldn't have left her.

But he had.

Yet, even after years of no contact, when danger had found its way to her, Rachel's first instinct had been to call him.

Because you still trust him.

"Hush it," she responded into her coffee.

The coffee complied.

Something moved against her hip, earning a knee-jerk reaction of nearly jumping out of her skin. Her coffee sloshed over the edge of the mug. "Sweet crickets!"

Even with the coffee and the soothing creek in the distance, she couldn't deny that she was still on edge.

Rachel finagled the vibrating phone from her pocket and shook some of the coffee off her other hand. The Caller ID showed Dane again.

"To be fair, I called to try and not scare you."

Rachel looked from the phone to the patio stairs.

On the path that led from around the house to the front porch stood Dane. Trying to look apologetic.

Rachel put her hand to her chest and took a deep breath.

"I guess I'm a little jumpy this morning," she admitted. Dane nodded but kept to the bottom of the stairs. He was still wearing his button-down and jeans, but now there were bags beneath his eyes, too. He hadn't slept. "Is everything okay?"

"Detective Foster thinks he found a potential lead. He and Billy are looking into it."

"Good." The faster the men were caught, the better.

Dane ran a hand across his jaw and nodded. "No suspicious activity was reported at Lonnie's by Deputy Ward and no one other than your friend came or went last night."

"Also good."

He nodded again. It was off. Like the motion was on reflex. Like he wasn't actually listening to himself. Rachel tilted her head slightly to the side, trying to figure out his thoughts. But, while she'd been good friends with the man years ago, it felt like a lifetime had passed between them. She could no sooner tell what he was thinking than she could tell what he was feeling.

"We'll keep someone on both today, but I need to go relieve Henry from Lonnie's until another deputy can step in," he continued. "His kid has the flu and his wife woke up with it, so he needs to hustle home."

Rachel felt herself perk up. "So you're going to Lonnie's right now?"

She already was turning with her coffee cup in hand.

"Yeah, just long enough until someone comes and relieves me."

"Can I come with you?" Rachel was positive it was exactly what she needed to feel better. She could either sit around worrying about the boy, or check on him herself. Maybe even talk to his uncle and learn a little bit more about his home life, too. Maybe set some of the rumors straight when it came to the teachers at Darby Middle. "I mean, I can take my own car if you'd like," she added. "I just— I'd like to see how Lonnie's doing."

Dane surprised her with a small smile.

"If you don't mind me stopping by somewhere that has coffee, I'm fine with you riding along."

It was Rachel's turn to smile. "I can do you one better."

THEY SET OUT from the house a few minutes later with two cups of homemade coffee, a Tupperware container filled with cookies, and too many things left unsaid between them. Dane had already known that Rachel asking to come along was a possibility, but until she'd asked, he hadn't known what he was going to say in response. He'd planned his day around sticking close to her while working the case from a stationary spot—which he'd gotten good at over his career as captain—so if she wanted to leave, coming along with him definitely made things easier.

Or, at least, the work side of things.

Their personal issues weren't as easy to work around.

So Dane decided not to address them at all. He was going to treat Rachel like just another civilian. There was a bigger picture. One he'd hopefully see when the men were caught.

He didn't need to, nor had the time to, get lost in the past.

"I'm surprised that Marnie girl didn't stay the night," he said once they were on the county road. "She seemed ready to fight by your side. Never seen a lady brandish a lamp before."

He kept his eyes on the road but heard the smile in her voice when she answered.

"You've seen a man brandish a lamp?"

Dane felt his smile pull up the corner of his lips. "Actually, I have."

And so Dane ate up the time between the outskirts of Darby to the other side of town by relaying the story about Marty Wallace, drunk as a skunk, coming into a restaurant to confront his cheating girlfriend. Who'd just happened to be on a date one table over. Dane had barely saved the new beau from receiving a whack upside the head by a fancy lamp when he restrained the cursing-like-a-sailor Marty.

"Want to know the kicker? After he got out of

jail, he went back to the restaurant and picked a fight with the owner."

Rachel let out a small gasp. "Why did he do that?"

"The lamp that he broke cost five hundred dollars. Marty didn't want to pay it."

"Five hundred dollars?" She whistled. "I don't blame him. I might have started a fight with the owner, too. Did he end up paying it or did he get arrested again?"

"Billy ended up feeling so bad for him that he talked the owner out of pressing charges." Dane couldn't help chuckling. "Then Billy managed to convince the man that the lamp was too ugly to be worth that much, so the owner went out and got a new one anyways."

Rachel laughed a good laugh. Dane hadn't realized how much he had missed the sound.

"That's our sheriff for you," he added. "A fearless leader with a bleeding heart when it comes to overpaying for lamps. I don't know what Riker County would do without him."

This time Rachel didn't laugh. He glanced over. Denim blue. Staring straight ahead.

"You know, I always thought you'd run for sheriff." Her voice sounded different. Off. Distant. "Wasn't that a part of your five-year plan?"

There it was.

One of those unsaid things. Dane fought the urge to tense up.

"I decided I wanted something different," he answered. "Now I can't imagine anyone other than Billy running the county. He's a good man and good at what he does. Plus, I like my job. I may not be hitting the streets as much, but I still get done what needs to get done."

It was all honest enough. His plans had changed and he was sure as sure could be that Billy had found his true calling. Dane, on the other hand, felt like he had found his in being captain. He might be a desk jockey most of the time, but he made it work. The only lie? It had taken a while for him to accept it.

"So what you're saying is that you stepping out of your office to do guard duty isn't on your normal roster of daily activities?"

Dane had to look over again. If only because of the humor he heard in her response. She was no longer distant. Dane was surprised. He thought talking about their pasts at any length would bring out the flash of anger he'd already seen several times in the past twenty-four hours.

"No, it's not something I typically do," he admitted. "I guess I just needed to hit my abnormal quota before the year ran out."

Rachel snorted.

Silence followed. It settled in the cab of the truck like pollen to the ground on a summer day. Dane kept his gaze forward as he navigated an older neighborhood. Darby wasn't the smallest town in the county, but it wasn't the largest, either. This was one of the three neighborhood clusters within the town limits.

It was also the oldest. All the strings of houses they passed revealed their age. Almost all of them showed disrepair, while some showed signs of renovation. It was also typically a neighborhood that housed a mostly older generation of residents. Not a popular children's or young family's neighborhood, if Dane wasn't mistaken.

"Does Lonnie live with his grandparents?" Dane asked. "I wasn't there when he was picked up and can't remember if I ever knew what his relation was to his guardian other than that his parents are gone."

"I don't know much about their family life, but I know he lives with his uncle, Tucker. His parents passed away when he was a toddler." Rachel's voice held a whopping dose of concern as she continued. "If you believe the gossip at school, his uncle views him more as an obligation than family."

He could tell Rachel didn't like what she was saying.

Dane didn't, either.

He kept quiet, though, and turned onto Amber Street. Henry's car was parked curbside in front of the house. Dane pulled up behind it and cut the engine. He didn't get out right away.

"I probably should have mentioned this before, but Henry's wife, Cassie, the one with the flu?" he started. "She's the one who took you back to the school yesterday."

Rachel sighed.

"That's just what I need on top of everything else," she muttered. "The flu."

Dane tried on another apologetic look and went out to talk to Henry. Deputy Ward was one of the newest additions to the department but, Dane had to admit, one of his favorite people to work with. Not only did he make Cassie, a friend and coworker happy, but he was a nice guy with a good sense of humor. Especially when it came to being a husband and a father.

"Sorry again, Dane," he said through his rolled-down window. "Cassie's sister is out of town…with my brother." He gave Dane an exasperated look. "The first time they decide to go on some romantic getaway together and my house breaks out with, as my lovely wife put it, 'exorcist-style vomiting.'" He ran a hand down his face. "If there was anyone else to help out, I'd call them in, but—"

Dane cut the man off with a wave. "Don't worry about it. Deputy Medina said she was more than happy to switch." Henry's eyebrow rose. Dane cracked a grin. "She got tricked into helping with courtroom duty, and we both know how much she hates being in there. For her this is an ideal way to spend the day."

"Glad I'm not putting her out, then." Henry motioned to the house. "As for why I'm here, no one has showed up or left the house since I followed them here last night. In fact, you're the only movement

I've seen all night and morning. Anything interesting happen at your place?"

"No, just the same."

Henry's phone buzzed in his cup holder. Dane spied his wife's name on the Caller ID. He laughed and tapped the top of the car twice.

"Go ahead and get out of here," he said. "We can handle it."

Henry nodded and was gone by the time Dane walked back to his truck. Rachel was standing next to it, a smile on her face and a container of cookies in her hand. When she looked at him, Dane felt like he was putting his feet back into that ice-cold water.

This time, though, it was different.

Soft blue eyes that had a life of their own met his.

For a moment they tricked him into believing that nothing had changed between them. That they were still close friends. That he hadn't dropped out of her life on purpose for years. That he hadn't been the reason her husband had been killed.

That, even if he tried to deny it, there wasn't something inside him that seemed to open up when around her.

But just like that, Dane remembered everything.

He remembered finding his best friend's body.

He remembered feeling Rachel quake in anguish against him after he'd told her the news.

He remembered the guilt that took root in his soul and had only grown through the years.

And most of all, Dane remembered Rachel wearing a yellow sundress, trying to change a tire a year after the funeral.

She hadn't seen him, but he'd seen her.

That was when he'd known he needed to keep the distance between them.

No matter what.

"Ready?"

Dane nodded and, despite his resolve, he followed.

Chapter Six

The two-story house was a mixture of dark and faded wood with a missing porch step and a patch of shingles in disrepair. The whole building seemed to be sagging, pulled downward and tired, but that might just have been an illusion from the way the entire lot sloped toward the road.

Rachel held the container of cookies to her stomach. She felt oddly nervous.

Traumas had a way of changing people.

She hoped Lonnie was okay.

"You might want to take the lead," Dane said, falling back by her elbow. "After what happened, Tucker Hughes might be more inclined to open the door to a friendly face."

Rachel shored up her shoulders and knocked. She wondered, belatedly, if Lonnie and his uncle had slept in—it was barely nine in the morning—but then she heard movement in the house.

"Someone just peeked through the blinds," Dane

said after a moment. "I'm guessing Lonnie, since it was toward the bottom."

A few seconds later the sound of locks turning came through. The door opened slowly but only an inch.

"Ms. Roberts? What you doing here?"

Lonnie's nose peeked through the crack in the door, followed by a suspicious stare.

Rachel shook the container in her hand.

"I was wondering if you had a sweet tooth like me," she hedged. Coming right out and admitting she was worried about the boy might make him defensive. She didn't want him to shut the door in her face. "It's the least I could do for helping me yesterday."

Lonnie eyed the cookies a moment before slowly opening the door the rest of the way. Rachel immediately knew two things.

One, the boy hadn't slept. Or, at least, hadn't slept well. His eyes, like the house, sagged. Second, she wasn't leaving until she talked to his uncle. For whatever reason she wanted—no, needed—to make sure he was okay. With an ache in her heart, Rachel realized it was the closest thing she'd ever felt to maternal.

"What kind of cookies?"

Rachel forced a smile. "Chocolate chip and oatmeal raisin. Both from scratch. My great-grandma's secret recipe, too."

Dane leaned in. "And let me tell you, they're awesome."

Lonnie looked between them. He seemed sold.

Dane stepped forward enough to bring Lonnie's attention back to him.

"How about you go get your uncle?" he asked. "Then Ms. Roberts here can wow you with some of the best cookies I've ever had."

Lonnie shrugged. "He's not here."

Out of her periphery Rachel saw Dane tense. She probably didn't fare much better. When he spoke she could tell he was holding back.

"He brought you home last night, though, didn't he?"

Lonnie looked bored, but he nodded. "Yeah, but then he said he had to leave and took off."

Rachel took great pains to hide her surprise. "Did he have to go to work?" Her voice was not as calm as she wanted it to be. She felt Dane's hand press lightly on her back. "Did he say when he was coming back?"

"Nah. He said he was going out of town and that was it."

Lonnie didn't seem to notice that both adults in front of him had gone from worried to angry in the drop of a hat. At least, that was what Rachel was feeling. Anger mixed with a hefty amount of confusion.

"Hey, Lonnie, why don't you take those cookies inside and we'll come in in a minute to have some, too?" Dane said. "If that's okay with you?"

Lonnie shrugged again. "Whatever."

Rachel handed the container over and then let Dane steer her off the front porch and onto the lawn. He didn't speak until the front door closed behind them.

"I'm going to hunt that man down and ask him why the hell he isn't here." He was fuming, his voice low. He pulled out his phone. "We still have his number on file."

"How did he get past Deputy Ward? Didn't he follow them home from the department last night?"

Dane ran a hand through his hair while the other scrolled through his contacts. "Yeah, Henry followed them here." He hit a number and gave her a severe look. "Henry has a keen eye and doesn't slack off." He pointed over her shoulder to the side of the house. An old truck was parked next to it. "And if I'm not mistaken, Henry told me last night that that was Tucker's truck. So if both of those things are true—"

"Then Tucker must have snuck off last night," she finished. "But why?"

Dane had straight steel in his voice when he answered. "I don't know, but I'm sure about to find out."

RACHEL TRIED TO keep an open mind as she went inside while Dane did whatever he was doing. Surely if Tucker had left Lonnie alone, there had to be a good reason. Maybe it was work-related. There had been many times when her mom had had to leave her for work when she was young, even when her mother hadn't wanted to. It came with the territory of being a single, working parent. Not every boss was understanding and not every parent or guardian could cross a boss who didn't understand.

But then Rachel was in the house and her open mind started to close.

It was a nice house. Sparse. Run-down but clean. She went through the foyer and the living space, and then into the kitchen, where she found Lonnie. Even before she saw him eating a cookie, she felt like something was off. It wasn't until she took a cookie in her own hand that she realized what felt wrong.

The house felt empty.

Sure, it had furniture, but that was the end of it. There were few to no pictures in the foyer and living room and just as many knickknacks. All the small details that made a house feel like a well-lived-in home weren't there. It just felt empty. Certainly not a place where a child lived.

A shell of what should be a home.

"I'm not dumb, you know," Lonnie said around a bite of oatmeal raisin. Rachel immediately feigned innocence. Was her worry and anger that apparent?

"I know you're here to check up on me."

Rachel quirked an eyebrow but didn't deny it.

"You didn't have to. I'm fine. Just like I said I was yesterday a billion times." He took another large bite of his cookie as if to prove his point.

Rachel leaned against the counter opposite him. She tried to look nonchalant.

"Maybe I just wanted to hang out with someone who knows how I'm feeling," she tried. "I mean, you said you're fine, but maybe I'm not. Yesterday was definitely scary."

Lonnie's eyes narrowed but he didn't take the bait. "I think you just came with that cop because he had to switch with that other one that was outside all night."

Rachel motioned to the cookies, surprised the boy had been so observant.

"Or maybe I couldn't sleep last night, so I made some cookies and thought you might like some," she countered.

The idea seemed laughable to him that someone might have thought about him unprovoked. That was clear in the look of disbelief he gave her. It pulled at her heartstrings. She decided to tell him the truth.

"You deserve more than a box of cookies," she continued. "Even though I never want you to put yourself in danger like that again, yesterday you showed a whole lot of courage when you attacked that man when he had a hold of me. Not everyone would try to help in the same situation, especially if it meant they had to put themselves in harm's way. It was selfless and brave. And I wanted to sincerely thank you for it."

Lonnie looked like he wanted to say something sarcastic. However he seemed to change his mind. He didn't acknowledge what he'd done, but he didn't lash out, either.

"Does your arm still hurt?" He eyed the bandage

at her wrist. He seemed genuinely curious. "Is it still bleeding?"

"I don't know, actually. Want to find out?"

Like with most little boys, Lonnie's intrigue tripled. He closed the gap between them to watch her unwrap the bandage. It wasn't bleeding, but it still seemed to impress him.

"That was cool what you did with the window," he said after they inspected the healing cut. "I thought you were crazy when you punched it."

Rachel laughed.

"You weren't the only one." They both turned. Dane was standing in the doorway. He had a smile on his face but it wasn't right, just like the house. It was empty. Off. "Lonnie, could I use your bathroom?"

He shrugged, keeping his eyes on her cut. "I don't care," he answered. Rachel lowered her arm so he could get a better view. It gave Dane the perfect opportunity to mouth a message at her.

Keep him in here.

DANE WENT PAST the bathroom and up the stairs as quickly and quietly as he could. Then he was in the master bedroom and trying his best not to curse too loudly. Tucker Hughes had been a mystery to him before because he'd had no reason to know the man.

Now?

Now he wished he had done his homework on Tucker.

Unlike the rest of the house, his room was chaotic. Like someone had ripped through it looking for something.

Dane stepped over discarded clothes and went to the closet. It was partially open and mostly empty. With a sinking feeling he did a cursory sweep of the rest of the room. He came up empty. Nothing pointed him to any answers as to why Tucker Hughes had up and left his nephew the way he had. Nor why he had seemingly packed most of his belongings. There was no empty luggage or bags that Dane could find.

He left the bedroom and went to the one across the hall. It was Lonnie's bedroom and while it was a little messy, it didn't look like Tucker had started or even attempted to pack up the boy.

It would have made more sense to leave with Lonnie than to leave him behind.

Though, again, neither course of action made sense.

Dane's cell phone went off in his hand. He hurried out of the room and back down the stairs. He nodded to Rachel as he passed the kitchen. Lonnie didn't stop talking.

"Captain Jones," he answered on reflex, closing the front door behind him.

"Cowboy Montgomery," Chance replied with a grin in his voice. Dane rolled his eyes.

"I'm not in the mood," he warned. It worked to snap the man out of any follow-up jokes or sarcasm.

"Why? What's going on?"

Dane paced himself right off the porch. Last time he'd talked to Chance was yesterday after Suzy had left him alone in the break room. He had wanted to tell Chance what had happened at the school. It was too much of a coincidence to have two pieces from the past surface, just as Suzy had said. Not that Dane believed it wasn't just coincidence one hundred percent. But, just in case, he'd told the man. They hadn't talked since.

"Just more things not adding up," Dane replied, skirting clarification. "Why? What's up with you?"

"Remember that guy I was waiting to call me back about the radio equipment that was stolen? Just got off the phone with him. Apparently what was stolen is specific only to someone who's trying to broadcast."

"You mean like air their own show?"

"Yep. They already have the means. Now all they need is the know-how. Then they can get on their own frequency, depending on how much they actually know. They can say whatever they want."

Dane didn't like that.

Why would thieves need to broadcast? "And you still have no idea where these guys are?"

"No. According to my contact in Birmingham local PD, the only lead they have is the van and Tracy Markinson. You know, the same van that could have been at the school yesterday."

Dane gritted his teeth.

"Just because two crimes happen around the same time doesn't mean they're connected," Dane reminded him.

"And just because two crimes don't make sense doesn't mean they *aren't* connected," Chance countered.

They were both right.

"Speaking of not making sense, I'd like to hire you as a consultant on something," Dane announced. "You interested?"

"Is it connected to what happened yesterday?"

"I don't know, to be honest, but it's definitely a mystery we need to solve ASAP." Dane could hear movement on the other side of the phone.

"Okay, got a pen and paper. Hit me."

Even though Dane was outside, he kept his voice low and walked farther down the sidewalk that led to the curb. As if Lonnie could hear him. He just didn't want to spook the boy. He'd already been through enough.

"I want you to find someone for me. Tucker Hughes. H-u-g-h-e-s." He waited a beat for Chance to write it down. "He's Lonnie's uncle. The boy from yesterday."

"And now he's missing?"

Dane balled his fist.

"More like he left." Dane relayed what he'd found and didn't find. "I already tried his cell. It's off. Can you tell me why he snuck out of his own house with packed bags but not the kid?"

"Sounds like running away to me," Chance answered.

"It sounds like Tucker Hughes knows something," Dane said. "And I'd like to ask him what that something is."

"All right, Captain, then let me work some of my magic and see if I can't pull this rabbit out of a hat."

Once their call ended, Dane took a second to let a breath out. He could feel a tension headache rising behind his eyes. Too many questions. Too many isolated events *or* too many connected ones that made no sense.

Yet.

Dane rubbed the back of his neck and looked at the houses around them. A car was parked in the driveway across the street. Maybe they had seen something or knew something. Dane pulled up Rachel's number and called her.

"I'm going to ask the neighbors some questions," he said by way of greeting when she answered. "I'll just be across the street."

"Sure thing, Mom."

Dane felt his brow rise.

"You're trying not to freak the kid out, aren't you?" he ventured.

"Yes, ma'am," she answered. "Anything else?"

Dane started toward the road. "Yeah, go ahead

and lock the door. There's something weird going on here. Stay on your toes."

"Sounds good," she said, voice chipper.

"I'll be back in a few minutes."

Dane was a second away from ending the call when Rachel responded.

"Love you, too. 'Bye."

The call ended. The surprise at Rachel's words and how they resonated with something he couldn't deny was pleasant within him, didn't.

Chapter Seven

Rachel talked Lonnie into showing her his art portfolio while Dane went to talk to the neighbors. It wasn't due until the end of the year, but she was surprised to see he had been vigilantly filling it. Lonnie was sitting on his bed trying to look like he didn't care, but Rachel called his bluff.

"These are really good, Lonnie. You must have worked really hard on them." She paused at a collection of doodles. They were in the style of a comic. She wasn't lying. They were really good. "This looks cool."

She held out the page.

For the first time since she'd known the boy, Lonnie's eyes lit up.

"It's not finished," he said. "I'm working on the other pages still. Then it'll be an entire comic book."

Rachel didn't have to check the smile that sprang to her lips. Any child expressing genuine passion for art made her happy. Add in the fact that that child had been written off by most as just an angry, unhappy boy? Well, that made it doubly wonderful to see him so enthused.

She delicately placed the picture back in the port-folio. "And what does your uncle think of all your art? Surely he has to be as impressed as I am."

Lonnie shrugged. "He's not into art."

Rachel was careful to put the portfolio back in the space between the bed and the wall.

"Just because someone's not into art doesn't mean they can't appreciate a good job," she pointed out.

He shrugged again. This time he didn't meet her eyes. "It's just not his thing."

"You know, I don't know much about your uncle," she started. "Why don't you tell me a little about him? Like what do you two do for fun?"

Rachel once again tried to get that open mind back, but she saw her answer in his eyes when he finally met her stare. Tucker was rarely home and they didn't do anything for fun. Still, she let him say it.

"He works a lot," he said. "And when he comes home he's tired. But it's okay. I don't mind. I like being alone."

A vise went around Rachel's heart and squeezed.

She didn't know what she wanted to say but knew she wanted to say *something*. Yet movement out of the corner of her eye turned her attention to the window.

A black Lincoln pulled into the driveway.

It wasn't a van, but the anxiety was immediate.

"Does Tucker have a second vehicle?" she asked.

Lonnie followed her gaze. "No."

"Recognize that car?"

He shook his head. "No."

Rachel looked across the street to the house Dane had walked to. She couldn't see him or any neighbors outside it. She pulled out her phone as the back door of the Lincoln opened. Tucker Hughes stepped out—or rather, he spilled out. Even from the second-story window, Rachel could see the blood caked across his face. He limped as he started toward the house.

"He's hurt," Lonnie whispered.

The front two doors of the car didn't open, but Rachel knew better. Just because no one got out of the front, didn't mean they weren't threats.

"And he's not alone," she said.

It was a moment of pure déjà vu.

Rachel went straight for Dane's number.

THERE WAS NO doubt that Tucker Hughes was in pain. Dane stood in the shadows of the house across the street and watched as the man wobbled to his front door. Whoever'd driven him stayed in the car. Dane took a picture of the vehicle and its tag.

Tucker knocked against the door.

Dane's phone rang. It was Rachel.

"Hide," he greeted. "Something's not right. I'm coming over."

"Okay," she whispered. "We're upstairs."

Her voice was so soft. Vulnerable. It moved Dane to action.

He called Billy. Sliding his free hand down to his holster, he crouched low and hurried across the street to the back of his truck. He'd had to park farther back, since Henry's car had been in the way. Maybe Tucker and the men in the car thought Dane's vehicle belonged to the neighbor. Either way, he didn't give it or Dane a second glance as he pulled his keys out and worked on the front door.

"Reed here," Billy answered. Once again, Dane didn't bother with pleasantries. Tucker went inside. Whoever was in the car didn't try to follow. Dane couldn't see past the window tint to get a description.

"Tucker just showed up, bloody, from a black Lincoln," he said, copying Rachel's whisper. "At least two people are still inside the car. Rachel and Lonnie are in the house. I told her to hide, but I'm going in."

"Be there as fast as we can."

Dane ended the call and slipped the phone into his pocket. If the passengers in the car were looking toward the other side of the house, there was no way he was going to be able to stay unseen while he made a dash through the side yard. But that was a chance he was going to take. Dane still didn't know what was going on. He could have been jumping to conclusions, but then again, his gut was firm in its assessment that something was *not* right.

Keeping his hand on the butt of his gun, Dane took a deep breath and ran.

No one shot or yelled or tried to get his attention when he got to the side of the house. He didn't pause to celebrate. Keeping low to avoid being seen through the first-floor windows, he looped around the back of the house to the porch. It wasn't missing any steps like the front was, but it wheezed something awful under his weight. Dane cringed, trying to make it to the door. The floor went from a wheeze to a wicked creak.

He wasn't surprised when the doorknob turned.

Instead he was ready.

Tucker's expression went from confused to afraid in the blink of his swollen eye. The gun pointing at him probably wasn't helping matters.

"Don't make a sound," Dane warned. "I don't want your friends coming in before we can talk. Got it?"

Dane didn't know much about Tucker, he'd be the first to admit that, but at least he knew the man wasn't wholly stupid. He nodded and retreated backward into the house, both hands in the air. Dane kept the gun trained on him. If he really was blowing this whole thing out of proportion, he was going to get a lot of grief over how he was acting.

But he wasn't going to apologize for it.

Not when Rachel and Lonnie were still in the area.

Dane eased the door shut behind him. Tucker watched, eyes as wide as they could go considering how swollen and bloodied he was.

"I'm Captain Dane Jones with the Riker County Sheriff's Department." Dane introduced himself. He didn't whisper, but his voice was low. "I have some questions." He started to lower his gun. "Okay?"

Tucker nodded. He kept his eyes on Dane. "Where's Lonnie?" he asked.

"Who are the men outside?" Dane countered. Tucker lowered his hands to his sides.

"Where's Lonnie?" Tucker repeated.

"Don't worry. He's okay. But judging by your face, you're not. *Who* are the men outside?"

Tucker shifted his weight. He threaded his fingers together. His gaze bounced from Dane to his gun and back again. He was uncomfortable and not just because he was hurt. Something else was bothering him.

"I need to know where Lonnie is," he said. "Now."

"You mean the kid that you left in the middle of the night?"

Tucker's lips thinned.

"I came back," he muttered.

"*You still left.* Why?"

Dane was mindful of his service weapon's weight in his hand and the space between him and Tucker. Was the man stupid enough to try to disable Dane?

And if so, why?

What the hell was going on?

A car door shut in the distance. With that, Tucker's weird behavior took another turn. This time it was straight to fear.

"They can't know you're here," he rasped. "No one but Lonnie is supposed to be here."

"That's not how it works," Dane said, eyeing the front door. "I'm not leaving until you tell me what's going on."

Tucker followed his gaze. It was like he was seeing a ghost.

"They'll kill me," he said simply. "They'll kill me if they think I called in the cops."

There was no more fear. No. It was worse than that. The man was terrified.

It made up Dane's mind. "You do *anything* and I'll take you both down."

Tucker jerked his head up to nod. Dane raised his gun to prove he meant what he said. He fell back to the doorway that led from the main hall into the kitchen. If anyone wanted to get to the stairs, they'd have to get past him first. Until then he was going to listen. He needed to know what was going on.

The front door opened without a knock. Whoever it was, even their movements into the house sounded aggressive.

"You're not thinking about running again, are you, Tuck?" The voice belonged to a man. It was deep, but Dane couldn't place it. It also clearly held no love for Tucker Hughes. "Levi might have given you a second chance, but I'm here to tell you there won't be a third." His footsteps slowed. Dane tightened his grip on the gun. If Tucker decided to give up his location, he'd have to fight sooner rather than later.

"I'm not running," Tucker declared. There was

more backbone in his voice than Dane expected of the man he'd just seen drowning in fear. The other man must have heard it, too.

"You're damn right you're not running." The other man spat. "Fool me once, Tuck."

"I'm not fooling anyone," Tucker snapped back. "I was just looking for Lonnie, is all."

"What do you mean you're looking for him? You're saying he's *not* here?"

"I didn't say that, I—" Tucker stopped. Dane hoped he didn't look toward the kitchen.

"I—I what?" Heavy footsteps barreled down the hallway. Dane held his breath, muscles tensing. "You know when Levi told me your part in all this, I laughed. Do you wanna know why, ol' Tuck? Because I couldn't believe the entire plan came back to you of all people." The other man snickered. "You buckle under even the slightest pressure. Hell, I remember how you quaked at every football game and you weren't even off the bench. Ready to cry if the coach even thought about putting you in. And now?"

Dane heard a soft thud and Tucker's intake of breath. The man must have hit him.

"Now I'm the only one who isn't surprised that you royally screwed this."

Dane imagined Tucker cowering on the other side of the wall. However, he was wrong. Tucker bit back.

"At least I'm not the one who got outmatched by a woman and a kid."

They could have heard a pin drop in the silence

that followed. Dane's own anger cascaded over him, coiling his muscles even tighter. His gut continued to grumble. Tucker wasn't just a neglectful uncle, he was a suspect.

"You listen here, Tuck," began the other man. His words had turned toxic, slithering around in a barely contained rage. Dane recognized the sound. Years ago he'd heard the same in his own voice. "For whatever reason, the boss thought he needed you to keep the boy safe. The operative word? *Thought*. The moment we caught you trying to get the heck out of Dodge was the moment you became even more useless than you already were. We don't need *you*. Not anymore."

Another sharp intake of breath let Dane know the man was getting physical again. Tucker whimpered. "What you *are* going to do for me is tell me where that boy is or else I'm going to kill you. Plain and simple. So make your choice. *Now*."

In Dane's head he was already turning the corner, gun ready, to keep Tucker from making a choice and to keep the mystery man from dishing out the consequence of whatever that choice might be. Planning ahead hadn't always been Dane's strong suit, but now, after what had happened to David, he tried his damnedest to keep two steps ahead of the game. Yet not even the most skilled of strategists could account for every piece on the game board. A lesson Dane was reminded of when something happened that neither he, Tucker nor their mystery man had planned.

A thump shook the ceiling.

The mystery man laughed. "Looks like I might not need you at all. Sounds like the boy is upstairs. Safe and sound."

Dane swung around the corner. "Don't move or I'll shoot!"

The mystery man didn't have a gun, but he did have a knife. It was an angry-looking thing with a blade that stretched at least six inches. It drew a stark contrast to the skin of Tucker's neck. All the man had to do was change his gaze to Dane and he was still in a position of power.

And he knew it.

After the surprise shook free, a smirk drew up one side of his lips.

"I figured Tuck would pull something," he said, all humor. "Other than trying to run away. And who might you be?"

Without declaring his intentions verbally, the man only had to press the knife to Tucker's skin. It held Dane and him both captive without the man having to utter any threats.

"I'm with the Riker County Sheriff's Department and you need to drop your weapon. Now."

The man was tall and lean and had a farmer's tan peeking out from beneath his plain T-shirt. His jeans weren't faded like Dane's but dark and new, like they'd just been bought, and his shoes were shiny enough that the reflection of the fluorescents in the hallway bounced off them. It was like he was a man caught between two worlds. Like he was still in the process of getting ready for a party or in the process of winding down from one. Even his blond hair was slicked back, yet he had a chin covered in stubble.

He also didn't seem nonplussed that a man of the law had a gun trained on him. He pressed the knife forward. Even in his profile, Dane saw Tucker cringe.

"I'm warning you," Dane said, pulling out his lowest baritone. Still the man didn't move a muscle or show any signs of fear. "Backup is on the way," Dane added. "And I'm here to tell you, you're leaving this house in either cuffs or a body bag. Those are your choices."

Dane took the smallest of steps forward.

It only made the man's grin widen.

Dane heard the creak behind him two seconds too late.

"There's always a third choice," said a new voice from behind him. Dane's blood froze. "Always."

Chapter Eight

Rachel kept one arm wrapped around Lonnie's body, fastening his back to her chest and his arms to his sides. She had the other over his mouth, trying her best to keep him quiet. She didn't like to get physical, but she also didn't like what they'd heard downstairs.

She definitely didn't like it when Lonnie had tried to run down the stairs toward the men who seemed to want him.

Telling Lonnie to hide in his own home when Tucker approached the house wasn't something he'd taken too well. He hadn't understood why they'd needed to hide. Rachel had still been struggling to convince him to hide in his room when Dane started talking to Tucker. Lonnie had, thankfully, quieted by then. Like Rachel, he'd wanted to listen to what his uncle had to say. So that was why they had been in the small hallway connecting all the rooms on the second floor when the third man came in.

Then Rachel had seen the same fear she felt reflected in Lonnie's eyes when that man had spoken.

It was the same sandy-haired man who had shown up at the school.

Rachel didn't dare move as three of the men spoke, but she heard every word.

So did Lonnie.

If Rachel wasn't so afraid that they would hear her move, she would have gone the few feet between her and Lonnie and pulled him back to his room. Instead the two of them stood in silence, letting the conversation below float up the stairs. Apparently their run-in with the man at the school hadn't been a stroke of bad luck on their part. They had wanted Lonnie. But why?

And how did Tucker play into it all?

Rachel had waited to see what happened next with bated breath until the man had laid it on the table. The bottom line.

Tucker was to bring him Lonnie or he would kill Tucker.

Rachel had shared a look with the boy after the violent directive.

Then she'd had to act fast.

Lonnie was going to give himself up.

Rachel had less than a second to meet the boy in the middle, throw one arm around him and cover his mouth with her hand. It was a plan that wasn't without mistakes. The awkward height difference between them pulled Rachel off balance. They hit the floor hard.

The men downstairs quieted.

Lonnie squirmed, but Rachel kept both grips tight.

The mystery man started to talk again, but Rachel couldn't concentrate on it.

"You're not going down there," she whispered in Lonnie's ear.

She needed to get them out of the open. If either Tucker or the man walked up the stairs, there wasn't a hope in the world that they wouldn't see them.

But then Dane joined the fray, sounding like the lawman he was. Together Rachel and Lonnie stopped fighting each other to listen.

Rachel's stomach went straight to the floor when another voice entered the conversation. The man in overalls.

"We're going to go hide," Rachel directed, careful to keep her voice as low as possible. "Okay?"

Lonnie nodded. Rachel wasn't about to roll the dice, though. She lowered her hand but kept her arm around him. Together they stood slowly and crept backward. She didn't realize she was still holding on to him until they were in his room.

"They're going to kill him if I don't go down there," Lonnie whispered. Rachel spun with her finger to her lips. "But—"

"You listen to me, Lonnie Hughes," she hissed. "*I* would die before letting those men get their hands on you, so you better—"

A yell from downstairs was swiftly followed by the sounds of a heated scuffle. Then a gunshot rattled the inside of the house. Rachel's heart squeezed with worry over Dane, but she knew he could handle himself better than Lonnie could if three men came upstairs after him.

Rachel shut the bedroom door and threw the lock. She turned around, surveying the room with new attention. The closet door was already open, but it was small. The window over his bed overlooked a small roof overhang, but with nowhere to go *and* if anyone was left in the Lincoln, they would have an unobstructed view of whoever went out there. The only place left was the bed. It would have to do.

"I want you to get under that bed," she said, bending to make sure he could fit. "And I don't want you to make a sound, okay? *No matter what.*"

More yelling from downstairs seemed to convince Lonnie to listen to her. He dropped to the floor and wiggled underneath the bed. Rachel grabbed the blanket and stuffed it under, too, running it along his legs.

"Here, put this in your pocket." Rachel pulled out her phone and slid it to him. "If we get separated for whatever reason, you call 9-1-1 when you're alone."

Rachel pushed the blanket the rest of the way under. She grabbed the sheet and pulled it half off, draping some of it over the edge of the frame. She hoped it looked like a kid's messy bed and that said kid was not hiding beneath it.

Another gunshot went off, followed swiftly by footsteps thundering up the stairs. Rachel whirled around, heart in her throat and adrenaline flooding her system. She had nothing to protect herself and nothing to protect Lonnie, either. If someone who wasn't Dane came through the door, she didn't like the odds.

So she made another split-second decision as she had the day before.

She jumped on top of the bed and fumbled with the window latch. Maybe she could recreate what she had done in the gym. Redirect their attention to stall for Dane and the backup she only assumed he had called. Though she knew she couldn't hide inside the room, the roof outside the window was flat enough that she could walk across it without falling.

At least, she hoped.

The doorknob started to rattle behind her.

"Hey, kid, open up!"

If her stomach wasn't already on the floor, it would have dropped to it. The voice wasn't Dane's. It wasn't Tucker's, either. Her fingers slipped, but she managed to unlock the window. The door behind her shook violently.

"Don't make a sound," Rachel said, hoping Lonnie could hear her. The dull ache in her hand became more pronounced as she placed both palms on the pane of glass and pushed up. Thankfully, the window slid up easily enough.

However, before she could use that in any way, a loud crack made her turn. She watched the old door split in two like it was made out of nothing but cardboard. Dark eyes met hers. They widened in surprise.

The sandy-haired man hadn't expected to see her—that was for sure.

"You," he breathed. He huffed as he moved some of the splintered wood out of his way. He had blood on one of his hands. Too much of it.

Rachel didn't need to see any more.

She turned and scrambled out the window like it was an Olympic sport and she *really* wanted a medal. The man yelled out at her, but she wasn't about to stop and listen. She crawled far enough away that he couldn't grab her unless he came out onto the overhang with her. If there was someone in the car and they were armed, all they had to do was get out and shoot her. Like fish in a barrel. Rachel didn't care. She just needed to distract the man. She needed him to follow her.

And follow her he did.

He just also changed her plan, or at least the gun he held up did. "I will shoot you in the head if you take even one more step."

Rachel held her hands up but stayed on her knees.

"Don't shoot," she pleaded. "I'm unarmed."

The man didn't flinch.

"Where's the kid?" he seethed, no smiles like he had worn the day before. He was hurting. Rachel hoped the blood on his hand was his.

"At the sheriff's department," she lied. "A deputy took him there a few minutes ago."

The man's nostrils flared. He was starting to fume. "You're lying."

"No, I'm not," she countered, rallying what she hoped was a sincere expression. She stuck as close to the truth as she could to make it easier to bluff. "We came to check on him and realized his uncle left him in the middle of the night. So we sent him off to the department until we could figure out where Tucker went and why. I was just closing up the house when you all showed up, so I hid."

Rachel had taken an acting class in college as an elective. It had been torture once she'd realized how bad at it she truly was. The unending scowl from her professor still haunted some of her stress dreams to this day. He'd always complained that her performances felt fabricated, like she was reading straight from a script. One time, much to her horror, he'd even told her in front of the entire class that watching her perform was like watching her recite a grocery list. One that didn't even have anything exciting written on it.

She'd once told David about that class, still experiencing mild embarrassment when a random memory sprang up from it. He'd laughed quite a bit before backing down enough to realize her feelings were hurt. Then he'd done what David had always done best and made light of the situation.

"It's because you don't like to lie," he had said. "So much so that I bet *that's* why you get all stiff when you're trying to be someone you're not or when you're trying to say something you don't mean. It's nothing to be ashamed of. In fact, I'll tell you what. I'm pretty proud of you for being terrible at it."

Rachel knew that what he said wasn't true—there were plenty of good people in the world who acted and didn't like lying—but it had made her feel better. She'd even started to be proud of the fact that she couldn't act her way out of a paper bag if she had tried. However, *now* she hoped beyond all hope that David's assessment didn't hold. Not today. Not when the man in front of her was so close to Lonnie's hiding place.

"If you don't believe me, call the department and ask," she added. "Tell them you're Tucker."

Rachel felt like she sounded confident. She just hoped he heard it, too. He was gritting his teeth hard. She could see the muscles in his jaw moving. A car honked in the distance. Dogs were barking a street or two over. What must have been only seconds stretched into what felt like minutes.

Within that time Rachel knew no matter what the man decided—to believe her or not to believe her—the outcome wouldn't be a good one. If she couldn't give him Lonnie, she was useless. If she could give him Lonnie, she would become useless right after he had the boy.

Either way, she realized there was a good chance she would die out on Tucker Hughes's roof. The thought should have scared her. Heck, it should have terrified her. Yet the fear that she felt around her heart wasn't for her.

It was for the kid who was hard to like but loved drawing comics.

It was for the captain who had answered her call without hesitation.

The man finally opened his mouth. Words filled with venom poured out. "We would have had him already if it wasn't for you."

Thinking he had been the cool one between him and the man with overalls the day before, Rachel changed her mind. He looked like a powder keg in the process of igniting. One who had pinpointed her as someone who needed to explode along with him. "This was supposed to be *easy*," he said with the shake of his gun. Rachel flinched. He didn't miss it. A smile broke through his anger. It sent a chill up her spine.

"You know, he might have been the endgame, but grabbing you was supposed to be a bonus if we could swing it. I think I'm going to go ahead and make an executive decision for the group." He readjusted his aim a few inches upward. Directly at Rachel's head. "This time we just couldn't swing it."

Rachel turned her head away. She squeezed her eyes shut. *I hope you're okay, Dane.*

A gunshot tore through the morning air.

Rachel waited for the impact, the burn. The end to a life that was filled with the good, the bad, triumphs and regrets. A life ended by something that made no sense out on Tucker Hughes's roof.

All she felt was something warm against her

cheek and then a small thud that vibrated through the knees of her jeans.

She opened her eyes.

Then she was looking at Dane.

Chapter Nine

"Rachel, I need you to keep looking at me." Dane holstered his gun as best he could while hunched over. "Don't look at him. Just look at me."

The "him" he was referring to was lying dead between them. Dane knew that without checking his pulse because he'd shot him in the head. It didn't matter if he could have helped them know more about what was going on. Hell, it wouldn't have mattered what he'd known, because the moment he'd aimed at *Rachel's* head was the moment Dane knew he wasn't taking any chances.

Not again.

Not with her.

Rachel listened. At least, only partially. She got to her feet but glanced at the man. Her face paled.

"Rachel Mary Roberts, you look at me and nothing else," he barked. It was a little too harsh, but it did the trick. Her blue eyes swung to him and him only. He reached out toward her through the window. "Just move a little to the right and then you're with me."

Rachel nodded and followed direction. Her hands were warm as they slid into his. Dane took it slow as he pulled her inside. Her eyes were wide. There was blood across her cheek. Dane knew it wasn't hers.

"Where's the other man?" she managed to ask. It came out with a waver. "Where's Tucker?"

"Tucker is downstairs. He's hurt but alive." Dane didn't like the next words he had to say. "The other man got a lead on me and ran off. I would have chased but…" He let his sentence trail off. He didn't have to spell it out. "Where's Lonnie?"

It was like someone had put ice down the back of her shirt. Rachel's spine zipped straight and she turned toward the bed. "Lonnie, you okay?"

The sheet hanging over the side shifted and then a blanket came out with it. Rachel knelt to help him wiggle his way out.

"Are *you* okay?" he asked, focusing on Rachel. "You're bloody."

Rachel started to touch her face, but Dane grabbed her wrist. "She's not hurt," he said. "But why don't we go to the bathroom and help her out?"

They both looked confused but let him lead the way. Fear was a powerful thing. Even if you didn't know what to fear, it had a way of making you move to avoid more of it. However, Rachel wasn't about to let Lonnie see the body whose image was no doubt burned into her mind. Dane watched as she kept at Lonnie's back. The last line of defense between him potentially losing a piece of his innocence.

Lonnie took a seat on the lip of the tub while Dane guided Rachel to the sink. She started to turn toward the mirror. Once again Dane stopped her. Their eyes met. She was close enough that he could see the few freckles across her nose. He'd never noticed them before.

She cleared her throat. "I'm assuming backup is on the way?"

Dane took the hand towel off the wall. He turned the faucet on and dipped it underneath. "Yeah, I called in the cavalry when Tucker showed up. I'm surprised we aren't hearing sirens yet."

Lonnie stood. Dane held his hand out in a stop motion.

"You need to stay up here for now," he warned.

The boy's expression hardened. "You said my uncle was hurt downstairs!"

"He is, but help is coming. What you need to do now is stay in here with Ms. Roberts and make sure *she's* all right."

Dane hoped Rachel was reading him. He didn't want Lonnie downstairs. He didn't want him to see Tucker. The blood on her cheek was nothing compared to what had gone down on the first floor.

"I sure would like the company, Lonnie," she said after a moment.

Lonnie didn't say anything but he sat back down. Dane turned to Rachel. She was searching his face. He tried to smile. He really did. But the contrast of the man's blood against her skin wouldn't let him. He almost hadn't made it in time to save her.

Dane took the towel and brushed it across her cheek. She didn't look at him. He didn't meet her eyes. Silence settled in the room. Dane continued to run the towel over her skin. Then, when he was almost done, their eyes met. He was so close he could almost feel the coolness from them. Two pools of the most crystal-blue water you ever did see.

The same water he'd known for years and yet not.

They were different.

The freckles were different.

And that was when Dane realized that something *felt* different. Past the adrenaline, past the excitement of trying to survive an attack, there was something that had happened within him. Getting a phone call from Rachel in trouble had been one thing, but seeing her on her knees, hands up in the air, ready to take a madman's bullet?

There it was again. Burrowed into Dane's chest.

Something had shifted.

Something had changed.

It prompted a truth from him. One that was more than just about that day.

"I'm sorry I didn't show up sooner."

It was simple and honest. The way Dane tried to live his life. He should have reached out to Rachel years ago. Hell, he should never have left in the first place. Being out of touch had caused a rift between them.

Dane had never noticed her freckles before.

And that bothered him now.

"You saved me," she said. She glanced at Lonnie. "You saved us. That's not for nothing." A small smile tugged at her lips. Dane tried to return it.

What was he doing?

What was he hoping for?

They were in an active crime scene, Tucker was hurt downstairs, one of their attackers was on the loose, Dane's phone had been smashed in the tussle and was of no use to them, and backup still wasn't there. And yet there he was, thinking about Rachel Roberts's freckles.

Dane cleared his throat.

"There we go," he said, tossing the towel in the sink. "You still might want to wash your face, but the bad part is gone."

"Well, what about *your* blood?" Lonnie chipped in. He pointed to Dane's right side. Dane didn't bother looking.

"You're bleeding?" Rachel asked, worry lacing through each syllable.

"It's fine," he assured her.

"I can see it," Lonnie continued. "Your shirt has a cut in it."

Rachel reached out but Dane was quicker. He put distance between them by stepping out the door.

"It's nothing," he repeated. "Just a little thing."

"But—"

Dane shook his head. "I'm going to go back downstairs to be with Tucker. You two stay here until I come back. Okay?" He gave Rachel another one of those looks he hoped said more than he could out loud. "Okay, Rachel?"

There were those eyes searching him again.

"Okay. Be careful."

If Dane had had Sheriff Reed's cowboy hat on, he would have tipped it to her. "Yes, ma'am."

"Son of a—"

Dane took in a deep breath.

"Don't be such a baby, Captain." The nurse gave the man a scowl that would put hardened criminals he'd seen to shame. "I just disinfected the thing. Not performed some kind of surgery. I didn't even put you in a room."

"I think you're lying, Nurse Bean," he said. "But I guess I'll let it slide. You are on your break, after all."

Nurse Bean rolled her eyes. As best friend to Detective Walker's wife and friend of the department's as a whole, the nurse had seen her fair share of them in her emergency room. Which meant she was more than comfortable giving any of them flack when they deserved it. Dane didn't think he did, but he wasn't about to back-talk a woman who might change her mind about him needing stitches.

Nurse Bean finished cleaning the cut and bandaged it, all while standing in the hallway outside the ER. She'd only seen him because the nurses on duty had had their hands full with a car accident, a cardiac event and Tucker Hughes. The latter was still in surgery. The first mystery man had done a job on him with the knife. The second mystery man?

He'd taken a bullet before getting around Dane and bolting out the back door.

It was still burning Dane's chest.

"And I think we're all done here. Now let me go get some butterfly bandages."

Dane brought his attention to the forefront. He turned just enough to get a look at the bare skin on the side of his lower back. It was a nasty cut, no doubt. Would have been nastier had Dane not been able to retrieve his gun. If the first mystery man had still been downstairs, Dane wouldn't have been so lucky. All he would have had to do was to use his gun on him.

Dane fisted his hand into the shirt he was holding.

Being in the nick of time wasn't a badge of honor in his book. It just meant that he'd only been able to get there during the last possible second.

And it didn't sit right with him.

"I'm guessing you still aren't a fan of getting doctored."

Two blue eyes with a smile hanging beneath them met Dane's gaze when he looked up. Dane tried to play off his anger. It made him compensate too much. He answered with sarcasm. "I just like hanging around shirtless in hospitals. Drives the ladies crazy."

He wanted to put his foot in his mouth as soon

as he said it but was surprised when Rachel glanced down at his chest. He wasn't a man keen on bragging about his appearance, but he wasn't above himself to know his weekly gym visits paid off.

"So *this* is where you pick up dates," Rachel responded with a snort. "And here I guess I've been doing it wrong these past few years."

She matched his sarcasm with her own. Dane hadn't expected it or her talking about dating. Even if he'd been the one to bring it up and it had been a joke. Still, the idea of her dating someone put a sour taste in Dane's mouth.

"How's Lonnie doing?" he asked, changing gears. "I haven't gotten a chance to really talk to him since we got here."

Rachel sobered immediately. She shrugged.

"Honestly, I feel like he's doing better than I am," she admitted. "He's been talking to me like all this is normal. Even with all this confusion, he's somehow managing to keep his feet on solid ground."

"Unless he's just internalizing it all," Dane had to point out. She nodded.

"There *is* that," she conceded. "I just— Well, I just want to help him but don't know how. I guess I just wish we knew more about everything that's happened." She lowered her voice and took a small step forward. There were those freckles again. Up close and personal for him to see. "Why do they want *him* and why am *I* a bonus?"

It had been an hour since the local PD and Billy

had showed up to the house. In that time nothing had been made clearer about the mystery men or their interests in Lonnie and Rachel. The only new leads they had seemed to have a pitfall.

They had the first mystery man, but he was deceased.

They had the vehicle that seemingly belonged to the mystery men, but so far it was empty.

They'd finally found Tucker, but he was now in surgery, fighting for his life.

And even if he did pull through and manage to talk to them, that didn't mean Dane was ready to trust the man. He had made it clear he not only knew about the men but had known of their interest in his nephew. Who, on an even more infuriating point, he'd left high and dry for an entire night before returning with trouble on his heels. Not to mention one of the men had said they'd caught him trying to leave town.

That surely didn't sound like Tucker had originally planned to come back home.

"I wish I knew," Dane finally said. "But we'll figure it out. Whatever is going on."

Rachel searched his expression, just as she had earlier in the bathroom at Tucker's house. She'd done it again when they first all bused together to the hospital, too.

What was she hoping to see?

And did he even want her to see whatever it was?

Chapter Ten

Dane wished Nurse Bean would hurry back so he could put on his shirt. He felt silly trying to keep a serious conversation going in the hallway. It wasn't a busy intersection, but he'd already gotten a few looks from the occasional wandering patient or nurse.

"So, what happens in the meantime?" Rachel asked. Her eyes stayed up to his now. "What happens with Lonnie? Surely he can't stay here. What if…what if Tucker… Well, you know."

"That's actually something I was coming to talk to the two of you about."

Sheriff Billy Reed looked more world-weary than he had in a while. A case always weighed heavier on him when kids were involved. It weighed heavier on all of them. Billy took his hat from his head and ran a hand through his hair. Dane knew the look, pulling the man's shoulders tense. They weren't going to like what he had to say.

"I just spoke to the doctor. Tucker Hughes is out of surgery and they're optimistic that he'll survive the night, but given the limited knowledge we have about the situation, I agree that Lonnie shouldn't stay here." Billy cut his gaze between them. "So I'll be looking after him until we figure out what's what."

"Why can't he just stay with me?" Rachel asked. "It's no trouble. I've got a big house with plenty of room for him. I wouldn't mind."

Dane was surprised or, maybe not, that she was so gung-ho to stay with Lonnie. They *had* been through a lot in such a short amount of time. Not to mention, as far as Dane knew, Lonnie didn't have any other family than Tucker.

Billy looked apologetic. "As much as I appreciate your offer, I don't think it's a good idea. If these men are after Lonnie *and* see you, Rachel, as a potential target, then having the two of you together might make another attempt at taking you both too tempting. So I'm taking Lonnie to an undisclosed location where I know he'll be safe. I won't leave his side. Neither will Deputies Medina and Grayson. Two *very* good people who are *very* good at their jobs."

The last part was for Rachel's benefit. Dane already knew and liked Medina and Grayson. They'd been personally vetted and hired by Billy.

"Lonnie will be out of harm's way. We'll make sure he stays that way."

"Well, then what about me?" Rachel asked. She was frustrated. That much was clear in the set of her furrowed brow and tone. It caught Dane off guard.

"Are you going to ship me off to some undisclosed location too?"

"No, I can't force you into protective custody or hiding," Billy said, not skipping a beat. "Though I *do* think it would be a good idea to find someplace unexpected to lie low at for a little while. Someplace our mystery men might not be able to find you if they kept looking. You could even, if you felt so inclined, bunk at the department. We have a second-floor room that's been converted to act as a place to sleep when needed. It's not the most comfortable place, but it gets the job done."

Rachel didn't like that idea. Dane could see that plain as day.

"She could stay at my place." The words were out of his mouth before he could think to stop them. "Again, it's not like many people even know where I live to begin with *and* Deputy Mills is down the road." Dane turned to Rachel. He was surprised to see her nod.

"If it'll keep me off those men's radar, I'm all for it."

Billy gave Dane a look that said more than he did out loud. "I wouldn't be doing my job if I didn't point out you need some rest. I know you didn't sleep last night." He motioned to Dane's side. "And now you're hurt on top of that."

Dane waved him off. "Nothing you haven't done yourself before."

The men shared a knowing look. It wasn't too far

back that Billy had put everything on the line to protect his then-ex, now-wife and their daughter. In fact, Dane could name a few more in the department who had gone over and above the call to action to make sure those they cared about were safe.

And he did care about Rachel.

True as true.

Billy sucked on his teeth. Then, slowly, he nodded.

"I'll let Deputy Mills know to keep an eye out," he conceded. With that he slipped his hat back on and nodded over their shoulders. Nurse Bean nodded back. "I'll keep in touch, Captain."

The sheriff left Nurse Bean to put the bandages on and inspect the cut one more time. Rachel stood silently next to them, watching. Even though she was within touching distance, Dane saw that her mind was a million miles away.

LONNIE WASN'T EXCITED about leaving the hospital with Sheriff Reed. He even told the lawman that straight to his face. Thankfully, Billy was a patient man. He took no offense while Dane and Rachel made a makeshift huddle to the side of the lobby, trying to convince him. It took a few minutes, but finally Lonnie agreed not to put up a fight. The twelve-year-old acted as if he had another viable choice. Even if his options were limited. But Dane liked Lonnie. He was confident and tough when it counted.

Though it was that toughness that made Dane

angry. Kids his age shouldn't have to be *that* tough. That was for their parents. For their loved ones. Both Lonnie was lacking for one reason or the other.

"You have that look going again."

Dane glanced over at his driver. The city of Darby was streaming by the window. Sunny, humid and turning into country. They weren't heading for Rachel's house on the outskirts. They were going to the town of Carpenter, following behind Deputy Mills.

"That look?" he repeated. "What look?"

Rachel kept her eyes on the road, but he could still see the furrow of her brow and the crease in her forehead.

"The look you get when you're trying to dissect whatever is bothering you. Like if you think about it long enough, if you focus *only* on that, then you can figure out how to handle it." She pressed a finger between her eyes for emphasis. "It's not good for you to use it all the time."

"I didn't realize I had a look." He smirked. "I also didn't realize I *dissected* things."

Rachel snorted. Dane didn't want to admit it, but she looked good behind the wheel of his truck. She'd said it was a non-starter that he do the driving when he was still in fresh pain. He'd told her he wasn't but then had tried to angle down into the seat. He'd been unable to hide how he flinched at the movement. The cut might not have needed stitches, but it stung enough to remind him exactly where it was and how awkward driving with it would be.

"Do you remember when you got your wisdom teeth taken out when we were younger?" she asked.

Dane groaned. "You mean when I ate steak on Day Two because I thought I was invincible? Then I got dry socket and had to take that godawful medicine." To this day the taste of it made Dane cringe.

Rachel chuckled and nodded. "That girlfriend of yours was *supposed* to pick you up from the appointment, but she bailed last second. What was her name?"

Dane groaned again. "Jennifer Hartley."

Rachel snapped her fingers over the steering wheel. "Yeah, that's her! She said she had a work emergency but—"

"But we found out later she was really meeting up with Tom McNolty," Dane supplied. "An investment banker in Kipsy with an awful goatee."

Rachel nodded. "I didn't really know you that well at the time. I think we'd only hung out once or twice. But—"

To the rest of the world, Rachel carried on with the next statement just as she had with the one before. To Dane, however, he heard the way her words softened ever so slightly. Treading near a memory. Being careful. In turn it made Dane stiffen. Not out of fear or worry, but out of anticipation. They hadn't talked about David in any context in a really long time.

"...then David called me," she continued. "He'd seen Jennifer in the city and knew you were trying to go it alone. And he wasn't about to have that. So he asked me to pick you up."

A whisper of a smile danced across the profile of her lips. They were a dark pink. Like peaches. Dane averted his eyes out the windshield. How could he be admiring her now, of all times?

"I still remember seeing you there. Sitting in the waiting room, basically stoned as you came off anesthesia, with gauze all in your mouth and still trying to talk to everyone. Do you remember what you said to me when I tried to get you into the car?"

Dane kept his gaze forward, but that didn't mean he was any less curious. He didn't remember what he'd said. In fact, everything from that day had been and still was fuzzy.

"I don't," he admitted.

Rachel sat straighter and pointed with purpose at him, her brow furrowed again. "I had just opened the door and was trying to get you inside when you turned to me and you said, and I directly quote, 'Thank you for saving my ass.'"

That earned a surprised laugh from Dane. "I don't remember that."

She joined in with the mirth.

"I figured you didn't." She laughed. "At least, you never brought it up again if you did."

Like a switch that had been flipped, her mood shifted again. This time Dane couldn't track where.

"Do you remember that you also didn't know who I was when I first came in to get you?" she said. "I had to get David on the phone to convince the nurse I wasn't just some strange woman off the street, trying to take you."

"I don't remember that, either," he said, honestly.

Rachel waved her hand at him dismissively. "Don't worry, my feelings weren't hurt. You were just having a hard time fighting through the haze of medication. Again, it's not like we knew each other that well to start off with. I think that's the first time I actually found out your last name. Still, once David did his sweet-talking to the nurse, I was worried you wouldn't come with me. I mean, you were a lawman, you thought you didn't know me, and your head wasn't in the best place. Yet..."

The truck slowed, coming to a four-way that was only a few minutes from the town limits. Rachel took the pause to look his way. She wasn't smiling, but she wasn't frowning, either. Dane tried to read her, to try and understand what she was getting at and why, but was coming up short.

"Then you gave me the same look you gave me in Darby Middle's gym yesterday. The same one you just had when you were thinking about, I'm assuming, the case. The very same look you're giving me now." Rachel let out a soft sigh. "You were trying to figure something out then. Trying to make sense of what you knew and fill in the blanks of what you didn't. You were trying to puzzle out if you could trust me." She shrugged. "And for whatever reason, back then that's exactly what you did. You got into my car, let me drive you home and then babbled nonsense to me once I had you tucked into bed."

She turned back to the road and kept on following Deputy Mills. "To be honest, I count that as the beginning of our friendship. Even if you were still hopped up on medication."

"I'm sorry I don't remember it," Dane finally responded. "I don't remember most of that day."

Rachel surprised him once again. She extended her hand and placed it on top of his. Every part of his body wanted to lean into the movement, into the warmth of her hand. It only made everything he was already feeling worse.

"The *point* of this walk down memory lane isn't really about Jennifer Hartley or a younger Dane Jones spouting hilarious nonsense. I just... I just wanted to let you know that everything can't be so easily figured out. Not everything has a straightforward answer and not everyone makes sense. And when you run into a situation like that or come across those people, you can't beat yourself black and blue trying to solve *everything*. Especially on your own." She squeezed his hand but then let go. Her demeanor didn't change again, but her tone did. It was harder. Stern. "Years ago a younger Dane Jones decided within the span of a walk from an oral surgeon's office to the parking lot that he was going to trust me. So now I'm asking that same man, do you trust me?"

Dane didn't hesitate. "I do."

"Good." She nodded. "Then trust me when I say,

with this case, don't do what you always do. Don't get lost in your own head and then beat yourself up when it's hard to find a way out. I'm here, you know. I want to help, especially for Lonnie's sake. So please, Dane, don't shut me out. Not again."

There it was.

Dane had finally run out of the distance between them that kept their past firmly in the past. If he'd only seen her at the school gym, he might have had a chance to keep avoiding it all. But now?

Now their paths were being forced together and here he was, trying to pretend he didn't like the closeness. That he hadn't missed her.

Maybe it was time to finally tell her the whole truth. The *whole* reason he had stayed away.

But could he?

"Rachel," he started, bolstering the courage even if he wasn't sure of what he was going to say. "Listen, I—"

The lights on Deputy Mills's cruiser came on, distracting their attention. He flashed his blinker and then drove off onto the dirt of the shoulder.

"Follow him," Dane said.

They were on an older county road, one of many that wove through the county. The particular one they had been on rarely had much day traffic. No one was in front or behind them and hadn't been for a few minutes. Dane instinctively went for his phone but remembered two seconds too late that it was as busted as busted could be thanks to his earlier brawl.

Whatever Deputy Mills had to tell him, it must have been pretty urgent. He jumped out of his cruiser and waved for Dane to roll down his window like his life depended on it.

"Turn your radio to channel 93.7," Mills insisted. "Now!"

Rachel put the truck in Park while Dane pushed the seek button on his dash. Each channel that scrolled by on the radio's small digital screen felt like a stab in his gut. A few of the pieces to the past forty-eight hours were starting to come together.

"What is it?" Rachel asked. "What's going on?"

Before Deputy Mills could answer, Dane remembered what Chance had said earlier that day.

"It's a broadcast," he proclaimed, guessing. "One I don't think we're going to like."

Sure enough, the first thing the three of them heard froze Dane's blood in place.

"—is finally here," a man's voice boomed through the truck's speaker. "It's time to pay the consequences, Riker County. Once and for all."

Chapter Eleven

"For those of you fine lawmen and women just now tuning in, I want to say a good ol' 'how do you do?' The sun is shining, the heat is cooling, and just because we have a bone to pick with you doesn't mean we can't be civil. So, let's remember that going forward."

Rachel stared at the radio like it could show her who was behind the broadcast if she looked hard enough. It was the third time the recording had played, fashioned on a loop. They'd been quiet while listening to the first one, but Dane and Deputy Mills had gone into action by the second. Now, on the third, Rachel was alone in the truck while the two talked together outside with Mills's cell phone on speaker between them.

"The time is finally here," the man continued. Like he was preaching gospel. "It's time to pay the consequences, Riker County. Once and for all. But what does that mean? What does that mean for all of you who have been singled out? Well, I'm here to tell you. Today a man, a good man, was killed in cold blood. His name? His alleged crime? None of that matters. But what does matter is the reason behind why the man pulled the trigger."

He paused. Rachel had already heard it before, but still she leaned forward in her seat.

"Power."

The skin of her arms erupted in goose bumps. Whoever the man was, he knew how to speak well.

"This power came with a badge and ended with a bullet in a good man, and I'm here to tell you that we're fed up with it. And we're fed up with those who stand behind that man and that badge. This isn't the first time this has happened, but it will be the last."

Now to the part that tightened Rachel's stomach.

"At least, it'll be the last for Riker County's very own Captain Dane Jones."

The broadcast extended long enough to hear the man's laughter erupt and then end. Shortly after, the loop started from the beginning.

Rachel looked out through the windshield at the man of the hour. Dane had his hands resting on his hips, attention on the phone between him and the deputy. His eyes had a hawk-eye intensity to them. He was focused, no doubt, and the look she'd just talked about was back in full force.

This time, she didn't blame him.

This time, Rachel couldn't help copying that same look.

She was no stranger to knowing how to feel when

people she cared about were in danger. It made you re-evaluate what you felt. Put things in perspective. Rachel turned the volume down on the radio and really looked at Dane.

Back around the time when Rachel had wrangled Dane into the car at the oral surgeon's office, they had been several years younger. Dane had been a new deputy then and on the wrong side of cautious. He listened to his gut before he listened to the rules and was more prone to jump into the fray than to stand back and make a plan. It was a series of traits that could have been career-killers or -makers, depending on how they were used.

Dane? He decided to turn his potential weaknesses into strengths.

He'd risen through the ranks until the idea of running for sheriff hadn't been so far out of reach.

By that time Rachel had easily called him a close friend.

But then everything had changed. One day Rachel had looked around and not only was David gone, but Dane was, too.

There had been many sleepless nights, unasked and unanswered questions, and feelings of abandonment on her part between then and now. Rachel wasn't stupid and she wasn't completely unsympathetic. David and the hostages had been executed during Dane's plan to storm the gate, so to speak, and try to save them. It had been his plan, his decision, and it hadn't worked.

But never once had Rachel blamed him for it. Never once had resentment or anger colored her thoughts of the man or the department that had backed him up.

The only person she had ever blamed for her husband's death was the man who had shot her husband in the head.

Rachel balled her fist.

She'd told that to Dane every time she saw another part of him draw away from her. She'd told them all that her sorrow wasn't their fault. A lot of them had felt it, too. But that hadn't been enough for Dane.

So Rachel decided one day to be patient. To let him distance himself until he could face her without feeling the undeserved guilt he obviously was drowning in.

Yet once he was gone, he never came back.

That is, until Rachel had called him in trouble. There had been no hesitation to try to help her. Though she couldn't say it was the same Dane she remembered. He was older now, and with that age had come experience. He had become captain instead of sheriff. He spent his days mostly behind a desk, only going into the field when needed. She would bet his gut still spoke to him, but he was more wary when it came to listening. And she'd be remiss if she didn't note the physical transformation was just as different. He'd definitely taken a shine to the gym. Even through his button-down she could see the cut of his biceps and the firmness of his chest. When he'd helped her off Tucker Hughes's roof and guided her to the bathroom, she'd even felt the strength in his hands. The steadiness.

It made her wonder how the rest of him felt, too.

The thought sprang up so fast that Rachel had to take a few seconds to process it. Had she really just thought of Dane's body? Dane's body against hers?

Heat traveled up her neck and pooled in her cheeks.

Rachel shook her head.

The man's voice on broadcast continued to ramble on.

Now wasn't the time to puzzle over her past *or* her future with Dane Jones.

All at once, Rachel made up her mind. She opened the truck door and walked over to the captain and deputy. They were ending their current call. It was easy to see that both men were a mile past concerned. Which only strengthened Rachel's new resolve.

Dane raised his eyebrow as she approached.

Rachel didn't let it sway her. Mirroring his stance, she placed both hands on her hips and hardened her jaw.

"So," she started, "what's the plan?"

"I DON'T LIKE this plan."

Dane was one of many in the briefing room at the sheriff's department. After the broadcast, they'd changed course. Since Dane was being singled out, there was a good chance going to his house was what their unknown broadcaster might want. Sure, he believed his house was safe, but that was before he had become a target. Now? He wasn't about to roll the dice.

However that didn't mean he was okay with the new plan Billy had come up with.

The sheriff gave him a knowing look. "Everyone in this room has, at one point during their careers, not liked a plan," he pointed out. "Especially when it involves them taking a step back."

A chorus of agreements swept through the room. Dane knew for a fact that some of them had complained about the same thing when their personal lives had been threatened. But that didn't mean he had to like it.

They wanted to not only bench him but hide him in a safe house. Or, really, hide them. Rachel sat next to him, back ramrod-straight. It wasn't exactly protocol to have her there, but sometimes the department had gotten flexible when loved ones were thrown into the mix.

Dane didn't even have the patience to think on the fact that he'd automatically lumped Rachel into the category of his "loved ones."

Billy held up his hand to stop any more guff.

"Let's refocus here," he said. "We need to put all our cards on the table and try to figure out who is holding what."

Dane nodded. He was right.

Billy leaned forward on the podium at the head

of the room. He motioned to the whiteboard. Dane was already up and moving toward it.

"It's almost like we have three cases running parallel to each other. Let's do facts only first and then we'll do theories." Dane picked up a marker and drew two lines next to each other. He started working on the first one. "Three men in a van show up at Darby Middle yesterday morning. They approach Rachel and Lonnie before chasing them into the school. Rachel gets creative, makes the men think they're gone, and the men leave. As a precaution I watch Rachel's house and Henry watches Lonnie's, following him and Tucker from here straight there." He paused to finish writing everything he'd just said. Everyone remained silent, waiting.

"The next morning—God, I guess *today*—" it felt like a lifetime away "—Rachel and I go to Lonnie's to relieve Henry and wait for Deputy Medina. That's when we find out that Tucker Hughes isn't home. In fact, he's packed up his things and snuck out in the middle of the night, leaving Lonnie alone."

This time there were grumbles from behind them. Half of the people in the room were parents. They were saying without doing so out loud that they would never have left their kids.

"While I go across the street to talk to a neighbor, a black Lincoln pulls into the driveway and out comes Tucker, beaten black and blue," Dane continued. "He tells me he wants to know where Lonnie is before we're interrupted by Knife Guy."

They still hadn't found out the now-deceased man's identity. Rachel had said she called him Sandy Hair because of his hair color, but Dane wasn't about to refer to the man as that.

"He doesn't like Tucker and is pissed Tucker tried to leave town. He says a man named Levi had given Tucker a second chance and that he couldn't believe Tucker was in charge of keeping Lonnie safe. Then he gives Tucker a choice—tell him where Lonnie is or Knife Guy kills him. That's when I enter, but so does a second, unknown man."

"Overalls."

Dane turned around.

Rachel cleared her throat. "He was wearing overalls when he tried to grab us. So I call him Overalls."

Dane would have given her a smile under normal circumstances—the name *was* cute—but the thought of the man trying his best to take her left a sour taste in his mouth. Still, he wrote "Overalls" on the whiteboard.

"Knife Guy doesn't waste any time in going at Tucker while I fight with Overalls." Dane decided to purposefully omit the close call of Knife Guy nearly gutting him or Overalls nearly shooting him with his own gun that had been knocked out of Dane's grip. "I manage to get a shot in on Overalls's shoulder as he flees. Then I run upstairs to neutralize Knife Guy." Dane didn't miss how his knuckles turned white as he gripped the marker. "Before that he tells

Rachel that Lonnie was their endgame and she was just a bonus."

More grumbles went through the room behind him as he made another note. This time it wasn't just the parents. "Tucker is then hospitalized and, while he's out of the woods, he's still not conscious, so he can't tell us anything. Though, to be honest, I wouldn't be inclined to believe what he said anyways."

Dane was at the end of the first line on the board. He switched to the second and wrote his name next to it.

"A few hours after we leave Tucker's house, Dispatch gets a call saying to turn to channel 93.7 and then hangs up. It's a lovely broadcast that talks about a man with a badge killing a good man and then point-blank calls me out." He paused and turned to look at Detective Foster. He had his notepad out. "And the call was traced to...?"

"The only damn pay phone still in service in downtown Darby," Caleb answered. "Detective Ansler is there now canvassing the area for any possible witnesses or working security cameras that might have gotten a good look at the caller."

Dane nodded and added the pay phone to the board. He hadn't asked about the call earlier because he'd already known that whoever had put the broadcast on the air probably wasn't stupid enough to call from a personal cell phone and keep it on them.

He would only be so lucky.

"We also are still working on finding the location of the broadcast," Caleb added. "Our friends at the local FBI office are spearheading that."

Dane drew a third line. He put four notes along it before capping the marker and turning to explain.

"Consultant Chance Montgomery approached me yesterday morning, before the incident at the school, and told me he was following a case about a series of thefts that occurred at the same time in Birmingham. Three warehouses reported missing shipments of dog crates, bubble wrap and radio equipment. Radio equipment *capable of broadcasting*. Chance followed it to Riker County because the van used to steal the bubble wrap had a plate that belonged to a deceased resident." He stepped aside to make sure everyone could see the name he'd written. "Tracy Markinson."

Rachel's eyes widened, but she didn't stop him to ask any questions.

"Last time I talked to Chance, he was still trying to figure out where that van went after Tracy passed." He looked to Billy. "He's also retracing Tucker's steps as best he can from where he fled last night."

Billy nodded.

Dane put the marker back in the whiteboard holder.

He didn't have to look at the notes. They'd already been blaring through his head since the broadcast. "*Those* are the facts as we know them, folks. I don't think it's a stretch to say that all cases are connected.

We just need to know how. So, now it's time to start asking questions." He smirked. "And I can't believe I'm saying this, jumping to conclusions."

Suzy kicked the group off.

"It sounds like Levi is pulling the strings," she said. "He's not just after kids. He's after Lonnie specifically. Considering Tucker, as far as we know, isn't the richest guy and Lonnie's only family to boot, I think we can rule out ransom. Since Levi also mentioned Tucker's job was to keep the boy safe, that could also mean we rule out any obscure revenge-type plans. And this certainly doesn't seem random. To be honest, it sounds like this Levi guy might be sentimental about the kid."

"You killed Knife Guy and then the broadcast happens a few hours later," Caleb interjected, picking up the conversational thread. "But if Chance is right, then they were planning to broadcast way before you even knew about him. Even before they showed up at the school. He either anticipated someone was going to take one of his guys out or you doing it made him change his message."

"Why need a message at all?" Billy asked. "A question that leads us right back to why Levi wants Lonnie in the first place."

"And why Rachel was a bonus," Suzy added. "Did they mean because she just happened to be with Lonnie both times? Or was she on the list with him, just not the 'endgame' as Knife Guy said?"

Dane wished he could answer *any* of the questions. Instead he looked to Rachel. She hadn't stopped staring at the whiteboard. Her expression was blank. A fresh wave of guilt went through him. She'd almost been killed less than a few hours ago and now there they were, talking about the unknown men, their intentions and their targets like it was just another day.

Which, sometimes for the Riker County's Sheriff Department, it was.

Still, he shouldn't have agreed to her coming into the briefing room. He should have let her take a break in his office. Dane was about to offer that spot in his office when she beat him to getting up.

"Can I write on the board?" she asked, hesitating for only the briefest of moments.

He nodded and stepped aside. "Yeah, sure."

Everyone quieted as she approached the board.

She took the marker and moved to the corner. She wrote quickly. Dane couldn't see it as she turned around on the spot.

"The gospel," she started simply, addressing the room as a whole. "The man on the broadcast gave his message like it was the gospel." Then she was looking just at him. Blue eyes almost too perfect to be real. "Dane, who else have we heard that sounded like that?"

Rachel stepped to the side. She'd drawn another line. Next to it read one name.

Saviors of the South.

Chapter Twelve

"The Saviors of the South effectively died with Marcus," Detective Foster said. "And even if it was some of the stragglers left over, that still doesn't answer why they want Lonnie."

Dane hadn't said a word. It was like Rachel had hit the mute button on the man. The sheriff was right there with him while Suzy and Caleb tried to disprove what she said. They were several minutes in and had gotten nowhere fast. Rachel hung out at her spot next to the whiteboard, trying to quietly piece together what the group was trying to put together aloud. After a volley of more questions between them led only in circles, she finally had an idea.

"If they are a part of the Saviors, then their interest in me is probably from what happened years ago," she pointed out. "The Saviors made me a widow and now this man Levi has, at least, some interest in getting me. Maybe Lonnie is somehow connected to what the Saviors did back then, too."

The silence that followed Rachel's words was

swift and calculated. No one disputed her, but no one agreed, either. But Dane *had* asked for questions, theories, and even jumping to conclusions. Rachel believed her thoughts fell somewhere in the gray area of all three.

Sheriff Reed took off his cowboy hat, placing it against his chest in thought. Caleb wrote in his detective's pad. Suzy rubbed her pregnant stomach while her brow drew in. Dane looked back at the whiteboard, eyes—and maybe thoughts, too—focused on something Rachel would bet none of them could see. Trying to puzzle out what was *really* going on.

Then slowly but surely, Dane's gaze shifted to hers. Rachel had spent years of her life around the man before the years without him had fallen. In that time she had learned his expressions, mannerisms, bad jokes and even brand of cologne. By proxy she also had memorized the color of his eyes. Or, at least, she had thought that was the case. She'd once thought of them as dark chocolate. Rich and smooth. Now? Now she was changing her mind about that.

Soot. They were almost as dark as soot left behind after a fire had burned its way to and through life. Something that, once touched, stained skin. Yet in a comforting way.

The sheriff finally spoke. "Whether or not this Levi man and his friends are part of the original Saviors of the South, a new wave of them or in no way connected, one fact remains."

Rachel didn't look away from Dane as the sheriff continued. She couldn't.

"They promise consequences. And from what we've seen just in the past two days, I don't doubt they'll try to carry those out."

Dane broke eye contact.

"So let's not give them the chance," Rachel said, simply.

To her surprise, the sheriff smiled. He slipped his cowboy hat back onto his head and addressed the entire room.

"You heard the lady," he said.

FIGURING OUT THE full motives, identities and whereabouts of Levi and Overalls didn't happen in the time spent in the briefing room. Not that Dane had expected them to magically find any answers just by talking about it. However, at least now they were all on the same page. Not to mention there were a few new leads to follow or already being pursued.

One of them being the possibility that the Saviors of the South were back. Which, Dane had to admit, wasn't too much of a stretch after listening to the broadcast loop as they drove out of town.

That didn't mean he had to like it. Just the possibility made everything in him pull tight, as if waiting to snap. When that snap happened, Dane had no idea if it would be his anger that came out in full force or his guilt. Either one was bad for his focus…and the woman next to him.

"I didn't know the sheriff's department had safe houses," she finally said, breaking their nearly half-hour silence. "I thought things like that were only in movies."

"This one isn't official, but we've used it a time or two in the past when we were in a jam. Do you know Suzy's husband?"

Rachel snorted. "Who doesn't know of James Callahan?"

Despite himself, Dane chuckled. James was the star of the smallest town in the county, Bates Hill. He was also the richest. Before Suzy, he'd also been the most sought-after bachelor. Even though they were raising several kids between them, and expecting one on the way, some women were still upset that James was off the market. Dane had seen the way James looked at Suzy, though. There was no doubt in his mind that he would only ever have eyes for the chief deputy.

An ache reverberated through Dane at the thought of their family.

He kept his eyes off Rachel.

"A while ago one of our own needed a place to lie low and he let them borrow a property he owned," he continued, gaze on the road ahead. "It was compromised, but he and Suzy saw the value in having a place or two that wouldn't be as easy to find. So he bought two properties and converted them strictly for hiding out. Only a couple of us, and I

mean fewer than five, within the department know
where they are."

"Is that where Lonnie is?"

Dane heard the worry throng through her words. It
was intense and heartfelt. It made him answer without thinking. "Yeah. He's at one of them, but not the
one we're going to. Even if both houses are off the
radar, we didn't want to chance having too many
targets together."

"But what about us?"

Dane tried not to tense. "What do you mean?"

"Well, aren't you a target now?" she said. "Doesn't
that mean we shouldn't be staying together?"

Rachel had a point. The whole reason behind why
they'd separated Lonnie and Rachel was to help curb
the temptation to pool whatever resources Levi and
his goons had to try to take both at once. But now
Dane *was* a target, according to the broadcast. Which
meant staying at the department might have been the
best course of action.

Yet, even as he realized that, Dane knew he
wouldn't have entertained the idea if it had been
brought up beforehand.

He wasn't leaving Rachel.

He just couldn't.

Dane shook his head.

"That's different," he countered defensively.
"We're different."

He hadn't meant the last comment, but it was true
enough. He and Rachel were adults, for one. Second,

Dane was a lawman. It wasn't like he was adding extra risk to the situation. He had a gun, knew how to use it, and would stop at nothing to make sure Rachel was safe if something did happen.

But that's not why we're different.

Dane opened his mouth to clarify but came up short. He didn't know how to explain something he couldn't make up his own mind about.

"We're friends," he decided to finally say. "And we stand a better chance of figuring this thing out if we work together."

Dane glanced over at Rachel. She took his explanation.

"Friends," she repeated.

"Friends."

Though Dane would be lying if he didn't like how final it sounded.

THE SAFE HOUSE was less of a house and more of a cabin. Small, cozy, and located at the beginning of several acres of old farmland, it looked like a page ripped out of a *Southern Living* magazine. From the pinecone and red berry wreath on the front door to the lone dining table's carefully arranged centerpiece to the hand-quilted throw across the bed, Dane felt like he'd stepped into his late grandmother's house. He resisted the urge to take off his boots at the door. Though he told Rachel how he felt about the small house. It made her laugh.

"Since when does Dane Jones read *Southern Liv-*

ing?" she teased, attention going to the small book-shelf across from the only sitting area in the place. "I thought you only subscribed to magazines about college football and how to build things with your hands."

Dane rolled his eyes and looked into the pantry in the corner of the kitchen. It was open with the living area. Only the small bedroom and attached bathroom had doors between them.

"You learn a thing or two when you date Becky Carr," he said with a laugh. "She was a hoarder when it came to that magazine. Had stacks of them in her house *and* her car. She even had us make our own Christmas wreaths from an article in one as a date. It was…an interesting experience to say the least."

Dane went to the back door, opened it and looked out before shutting it and throwing the lock. He turned back to Rachel, wondering if she'd heard him. He was met with a raised eyebrow and a look he couldn't read. It turned into a grin as she dropped onto the love seat.

"You're dating Becky Carr? As in the Becky who runs the florist shop in Carpenter? The same Becky who nicknamed herself Hardy Carr-Carr?"

Dane threw his head back as a laugh came out uninhibited.

"I'd forgotten she called herself that," he said, dropping into a chair next to the couch. It was such a close proximity that he had to be mindful of his knees not touching hers. "But no, we're not still dating. That ended a few years ago."

"Oh, too bad." Rachel picked up one of the coffee table books. A picture of something craft-related was on the cover. "Was it serious?"

Dane couldn't help raising his brow at that. Then again, it wasn't unusual for Rachel to pry into his romantic life. She'd tried to play matchmaker for him multiple times when they were younger.

They *were* friends. They'd just covered that, after all.

Yet Rachel wouldn't meet his eyes.

"Not exactly," he admitted. "Suzy introduced me to her because she said I was becoming a hermit and it was 'alarming.'" Dane snorted. "We only went on a few dates. Honestly, I think she was more interested in the *idea* of dating someone in law enforcement and not actually dating someone in law enforcement. She actually tried to give an ultimatum when I had to cancel a date to go to a crime scene. Said it was either her or the job."

That earned a look of surprise from Rachel. "No, she didn't."

Dane laughed and held up two fingers. "Scout's honor."

"Considering you're now a captain at the sheriff's department, I'm assuming you let her down gently."

Dane nodded but winced. "I might have gotten overly defensive about it and come off a little too blunt, though. Said some things I'm not entirely proud of. To this day Suzy gives me guff about it. But Becky started dating her now-husband after that. Has a couple of kids running around and seems happy enough. I just can never buy flowers in Carpenter again."

They shared a laugh and, for a moment, Dane felt the walls he'd had up around Rachel start to lower. Could they really pull off being friends again? Did he want to? Was it even possible?

"How about you?" he asked. "Seeing anyone?" Dane had meant it to be casual, but somehow it sounded off.

Rachel put the book back on the coffee table and shook her head. "I haven't been on a proper date in almost two years." She managed to look sheepish. "Do you remember Tatum Rogers?"

Dane was already shaking his head. But not because he didn't remember the man. "Don't tell me you went out with Tatum Rogers." Dane was holding back a laugh the best he could. It was Rachel's turn to cringe. "Ha! How can you give me any flack about Hardy Carr-Carr when you went out with Tatum Talks-About-Himself-in-the-Third-Person Rogers?"

Rachel was off the couch and waving a hand at him.

"He didn't *always* talk about himself in third person," she proclaimed halfheartedly. "He only did it when he was really excited about something."

Dane got up and followed her into the kitchen. "Rachel, talking about yourself once in third person is too much already. Please tell me it was you who called it off."

She opened the pantry and went directly for a box of pasta noodles. He was suspicious when she didn't answer right away. "Rachel…?"

"Fine, he broke up with me."

Dane was afraid that he'd touched a nerve until she sighed.

"And he did it in third person, too."

Dane couldn't stop himself from laughing.

"Get it all out," Rachel said. "I'll just make us something to eat while you make fun of me. Deal?"

Dane just kept on laughing.

"I THINK IT's time to go."

Levi looked around the garage. He didn't want to leave anything behind. At least, nothing they weren't *supposed* to leave. Making sure not to touch anything, he made one more sweep. The garage wasn't necessarily large, but it wasn't small, either. There was enough room to make a mistake. And he'd be damned if he'd be the one to make it.

"How long will this keep going?" Javier asked, motioning to the radio equipment. "How long will it keep playing?"

Levi rolled his eyes. He didn't like Javier, hadn't liked him from the start. But he was another set of hands and muscle. He'd already lost Wyatt that morning. Plus, Chet had been wounded. What had started as a well-manned group had shrunken in the span of one day. By the end of this thing, Levi might be the one holding all the strings.

"It'll keep going until it's manually shut down," he said. "*But* they have to find this place first."

Javier nodded and grabbed his bag. A semiautomatic was housed inside it. Levi hoped Javier was better at shooting than he was at thinking.

"What if they do? What if they find this place?"

"Then we better not be here. So let's stop yapping and get out."

Javier wasn't the least bit worried about double-checking his area, so Levi did it for him. Even though he had no problem with the dense man getting caught, Levi believed that if the FBI got Javier he would try and make a deal with them. Levi outranked Javier, Wyatt and Chet with what he knew but if Javier started talking he could still do some damage. Especially to Levi. He hadn't bothered hiding his identity from the ex-bouncer.

Levi was going to have to kill him when everything was said and done anyway.

The drive to the house was uneventful. Javier kept quiet in the back seat with his gun and Levi didn't try to start anything. They both knew what happened next. They'd certainly planned it long enough to be confident.

Levi parked the car and helped Javier take their gear inside. The house was cold. He hated the heat.

"Honey," he sang, high-pitched and mockingly. "I'm home!"

Javier snickered but was wise to stay quiet. He scooped up the cat and disappeared into the next room. The man in the office wasn't as amused.

"If he sees you acting like an idiot, he'll only continue to act like an idiot." The man looked up from his newspaper and gave Levi a look that said he wasn't impressed.

Levi turned and shut the door. "I think that ship has sailed already."

The man sighed. "Whether or not that's true, it doesn't matter now, does it?"

"Either way we get what we want," Levi said. "Well, if the plan works, that is." Levi tensed. He knew he was taking a risk, but he had to voice his concerns. He continued when the man didn't respond. "What if you can't get him? What if you can't grab the boy?"

Marcus smiled. "Then I'll grab her."

Chapter Thirteen

The steam filled the bathroom while tears filled Rachel's eyes. Thanks to Suzy and her husband restocking the house before they arrived, she and Dane had spent an hour or so eating homemade mac 'n' cheese and catching up like old friends. From disastrous dates to career moves and thoughts on gossip new and old, they'd found a way to make the cabin's kitchen into a time machine.

It had been nice.

And had made Rachel forget why they were there.

At least, until she'd gone into the shower.

There, beneath the stream of hot water, she had remembered the men. Remembered how they'd grabbed her. How they'd terrified her.

How one of them had almost killed her.

And how he had, instead, died in front of her.

Rachel had done what Dane had told her. She'd looked into his eyes and followed them until she had been no longer on the roof and safely inside Lonnie's room. But there had been the first moment after it had happened when Rachel had looked down at the man dead near her feet. His eyes had been open, staring at nothing.

Then there was the blood.

Rachel had cradled her cheek in the shower. The tears had been slow at first and then had walloped her. She'd held one hand over her mouth and used the other to hold herself up against the wall. Part of her was afraid that Dane would hear her and run in to comfort her. Part of her wanted that.

Which seemed to make the emotions spilling out of her even worse.

After everything that had happened, there she was, thinking about Dane, when less than two days ago just the thought of him had made her angry.

"Prioritize," Rachel told the mirror. She wiped the condensation aside and then scrubbed her hands beneath her eyes. They were red and swollen.

She sighed.

There was no hiding the fact that she had been crying.

She dressed quickly into the pajama set and underwear that, Rachel assumed, Suzy had purchased and put out for them. It was definitely a step up from the baggy tee and loose shorts she often slept in at home. It oddly fit like a glove, too.

Rachel took one last look at her too red eyes, pulled her hair into a quick, messy braid, and tried to pretend everything was okay as she left the bathroom.

Dane's voice was quiet but insistent. Rachel

paused, worry starting to make her muscles seize up, but she never heard another voice. He must have been on the phone. She walked to the bedroom door. She'd left it open, not liking the idea of having two doors closed between them, and peeked out around the door frame.

Once again Rachel was met with an uninhibited view of Dane Jones. Sitting on the couch, he had a notebook open on his lap and the phone to his ear. The other hand held his chin, propped up on his knee. His brow was drawn and his jaw set hard.

He was in work mode.

He was so handsome.

The thought sprang up just as heat moved from below her waist. It started to travel upward, turning into a full-body blush. Rachel took a step back, worried Dane would somehow know what she was feeling. Instead, the quick movement alerted the captain to her presence.

Two dark eyes nearly swallowed her whole.

He smiled but held a finger up to tell her to hold on.

Rachel nodded. She swallowed when he looked back at his notebook.

"Yeah, Chance, thanks for this," he said into the phone. "I'll look into it… Yeah, should be no problem here… Yeah, just call this number." He laughed. "I guess I lucked out with this burner phone, huh? Good thing we had it at the department." Something serious must have been said on the other end of the conversation. Dane sobered. "I will, brother. Thanks."

Rachel went to the chair and sank into its fabric after he ended the call.

"Was that Chance the cowboy?" she asked. The burn from her blush was ebbing away. Dane nodded, his focus switching to the notebook. Rachel couldn't see what it said, but half the page was filled.

"I can't believe you even remember Chance," he said. "You two only met once or twice, right?"

"Hey, you never forget your first cowboy. Even if you just meet him in passing."

Dane kept his gaze on the notebook, but he snorted. "He's definitely something when it comes to first impressions."

Rachel waited for him to say more. When he didn't, she continued. "Remind me to ask Suzy if she'd be interested in being a personal shopper. She guessed my size perfectly. Did she shop for you, too?"

Dane snorted again. "She didn't shop for us. James's friend and head of security did. Yeah, I know. It blew Suzy's mind that a man could find the—and I quote, 'perfect pair of jeans.' When she and James were in a tough spot a while back, he helped them out by buying some things she needed. Last I heard, Suzy was still begging him to help her out. Something about trying to find the perfect pair of boots to go with her jeans."

The whole time Dane spoke, Rachel could see his

eyes scanning the writing on the paper. He was trying to solve their current predicament while keeping her entertained. It made her feel useless and stopped any normal response from coming out.

Dane noticed the hesitation. He looked up.

It must have been the first time he really looked at her. His gaze swept across her face and stopped at her eyes. Like a match had been struck, a look of such acute concern blazed across his expression.

It wasn't like she hadn't known he'd notice that she'd been crying.

It wasn't like he hadn't seen it before.

Yet he didn't say anything. At least, not about that. "Do you want some cookies?"

It was such an off-the-wall question that Rachel laughed. Dane's expression softened and an almost-wicked grin appeared as he rose off the couch. "I may have laid on the 'I'm a target' thing a little too thick with Suzy when I asked if she could add Oreos to the shopping list for this place."

"But the important question is, did you—?"

Dane held up his hand to silence her. She watched quietly as he opened the refrigerator. He pulled out a small jug of milk.

"My hero."

Dane's grin grew. "When it comes to dessert, always."

She kept to her chair as he got out a plate and filled it with cookies. He placed it in front of her before fixing them two cups of milk. They didn't talk until they both were seated and had one milk-soaked cookie in.

"So, did Chance find anything helpful?" Rachel asked. "Are there any new leads?"

Dane let out an exhale that was long but didn't deflate his posture. He eyed his notebook before answering.

"Yes and no," he said. "He found out what happened to Tracy Markinson's van after he passed. Apparently it was given to a family friend who used it to help move a local construction company's equipment for out-of-town jobs. They ended up not using it as much as they thought they would, so never bothered changing the tag. The owner ended up letting a friend use it to haul things around his farm and his acreage for a few years. He didn't change the tag again, since the van only stayed on his property. *Then* one night it was stolen. It didn't reappear until it was spotted on security cameras leaving the warehouse in Birmingham."

"So, no lead but—"

"A mystery we can cross off the list," he finished.

Rachel dunked another cookie. She twirled it thoughtfully over the cup so it didn't drip. "Did he have any idea about why they took bubble wrap and dog crates?"

Dane shook his head. "He's still looking into that, but I'm not convinced it wasn't just a way to throw us off track."

"And Tucker?" Rachel felt a wave of anger at the

man for leaving Lonnie behind when he had tried to run. "Any word on where he went after he left the house? Any change on his condition in the hospital?"

Dane shook his head again and put an Oreo in his mouth. It was the most thoughtful she'd ever seen someone look while eating a cookie before.

"No and no. Tucker still isn't conscious."

They ate the remaining cookies in silence. Rachel recognized that the captain had retreated into his thoughts. She joined him, trying to answer *something* with the limited information they had, but it didn't work.

"Have you ever had so many questions in your head you feel like you're going to explode?" she finally said. "Can you combust because of confusion?"

Dane let out another long sigh. A small smile tugged at the corner of his lips. "If you can, I think I would have by now." He flipped his wrist up to check his watch. "Okay, so I wasn't going to say anything, but I think it's high time I took a shower. This place is too small for me to wait until tomorrow."

Rachel stood with him and collected their dishes, waving him off. "Go on ahead. I've got it from here."

Dane gave her a slightly stronger smile and disappeared into the small bathroom.

Rachel cleaned up the little mess they had managed to make. She paused as she folded the blanket on the couch.

Really, it was a love seat.

And it was much too small for anyone to sleep on.

Rachel turned to look through the open doorway that led into the bedroom. A single butterfly dislodged itself in her stomach and continued to flutter around until Dane was clean and back to his notebook. It stayed flying around while she excused herself to brush her teeth and it kept up its flight path as she padded back to that same open door, but now looking out from the room.

"Hey, Dane?" she called, trying her best to keep her voice from giving her nerves away. "I think I'm going to call it a night, if that's okay?"

Dane looked up and nodded. The bags that had been beneath his eyes that morning had darkened considerably. Worry pushed aside her trying to remain nonchalant. She put her hands on her hips and narrowed her eyes. "And I'm here to tell you that it's your bedtime, too, Captain. You look like you're two seconds from passing out as it is."

Dane opened his mouth. Rachel wasn't having it. "You stayed up all last night to make sure I was safe. If you don't sleep here, it will only make me feel like even more of a burden. And you said it yourself. Not many people know about this place. Plus, I'm a light sleeper. If someone comes and breaks in, I should hear them."

Rachel fully expected to keep arguing. However, Dane surprised her.

"Okay." He put his notebook down and ran a hand across his face. "I guess sleeping a few hours might do me some good. Which might do this case some good. Who knows? Maybe some clue might shake loose in a dream."

Rachel laughed. "That's the spirit." That butterfly began an even more sporadic dance. She swallowed and pasted on a smile. "You can sleep in here with me," she said. "There's more than enough room and you've more than earned a comfortable place to rest your head after the past two days."

Dane must have been more tired than Rachel thought. After only a moment or two of hesitation, he stood.

"Okay," he said. "Thanks."

"It's nothing," she told him. "But let it be known, I get the right side. Otherwise that's a nonstarter."

Dane gave her a look that made the heat in her body start to pulse. When he answered, it was a deep, smooth sound.

"Yes, ma'am."

THAT HEAT OF the shower had pulled out whatever alertness Dane had had left. What made him sharp in the field or behind the desk at work must have dulled because of it. Not to mention, he *was* tired and not just physically. Trying to pull together the several threads of what was going on to make one cohesive piece had been draining. Especially when he had realized Rachel wasn't as okay as she had let on. Her swollen eyes were testament to that. But the heat of the shower, exhaustion and frustration couldn't account for why he was now in bed with the same woman.

No, that was something else.

Something Dane shouldn't have given in to. No matter how small the couch was.

"It's not like we've never slept together before."

Dane opened his eyes. He was on his side, facing Rachel. He hadn't wanted to sleep on his wound. The soft light from beneath the closed bathroom door was bright enough that he could see the shine of her eyes and the outline of her side beneath the covers but not much more. "When you helped me pick up that bed frame from my mom's house up north? And we had to stop in that crummy motel and spend the night because of the storm on the way back? Remember?"

Dane did. It had been almost a year after David had passed. Rachel had decided to get a smaller mattress and her mother had offered her a bed frame for it. Dane had offered to use his truck to help her haul and move it.

"Calling it 'crummy' is a lot more generous than what I would have described it as," he said. They had almost slept in the truck, but Rachel had been too nervous with the storm raging outside. So they'd slept in their clothes. Jackets and shoes, too.

"My point is, you don't have to be so tense," she added. "We're just two tired adults who have had one helluva weekend. Got it?"

Dane smiled even though he doubted she could see it.

"I'll try to loosen up," he promised. "Just as long as you try not to snore like you did last time."

A soft fist landed against his shoulder.

"Hey, now. I told you, I don't snore."

"Whatever you say."

Rachel laughed but didn't try to deny it any further. Dane closed his eyes as they both lapsed into silence. Slowly he tried to let himself relax, but their small trip down memory lane had had a polarizing effect on him. On the one hand, it brought back memories of the two of them before he'd decided to distance himself. Just like they had been earlier, back when they were good friends. Comfortable around each other and able to enjoy even the most mundane things together. On the other hand, it highlighted the differences between their impromptu motel stay and the impromptu sleepover they were having now.

Back then Dane hadn't noticed the freckles on Rachel's cheeks.

Now he could see them with ease just from memory.

Back then he had fallen asleep talking to her.

Now there was a silence that felt heavy in the room around them.

Back then there had been layers of clothes and jackets between them with a king-size bed giving them distance from each other.

Now?

Now Dane was doing his best not to think about Rachel's body so close to his that he could feel the heat from her pressing against the front of him. How she was so close he could smell the soap from her skin and the shampoo from her hair. How, even though his mind was saying no, his arms wanted to be around her, pulling her against him so that he could protect her even in sleep.

How another part of him pointed out he also wanted to *not* sleep with her at the same time.

Dane wrestled with his body and mind for what felt like hours, trying to figure out which was stronger, until finally something made his decision for him.

The sound of Rachel's even breathing filled the bedroom. She was asleep.

"Good night, Rach," Danc whispered.

And just like that, Dane followed her into unconsciousness.

Chapter Fourteen

Rachel awoke with a start. Not because of any noise or some other terrifying thing that had pulled her from sleep. No, instead, she'd figured something about the case out. Or, rather, remembered it thanks to a stress dream about being back in high school.

She opened her eyes as a jolt of excitement started to push the fog of sleep from her head. Even though she'd had a breakthrough, it still took her a few seconds too long to remember she wasn't in her bed. Not even in her house. Instead she was somewhere foreign. A pleasant heaviness surrounded her. It was soft against her cheek and radiated warmth down her front.

Rachel blinked several times until what she was looking at filtered in. It was Dane. And not only was it Dane, it was his collarbone she was staring at. Her cheek wasn't just on something soft, it was resting on top of his biceps.

Rachel froze as she took stock of the rest of her position. Not only was she lying on top of his arm, she was fully tucked into his sleeping embrace. As if she'd been drawn directly into his chest after falling asleep, forcing him to put one arm beneath and around her while the other was slung over her hip. Her hands were against her chest, but that did little to diminish the rest of their bodies' closeness.

Rachel's breath caught as Dane shifted the arm over her slightly. From one butterfly in her stomach the night before, hundreds had multiplied. Dane was just so warm, a detail that started a different surge of excitement within her.

Rachel tipped her head up as slowly as possible, trying to get a glimpse of his face. All she could see was the stubble beneath his chin and along his jaw. So she listened to his breathing to confirm he was still asleep and decided to take a moment to calm down.

And that was what being in Dane's arms was doing.

It was a place of comfort, of safety.

It was a place of longing.

It was unexpected.

Rachel closed her eyes and focused on the heat of his skin against her cheek. It was nice, sure, but it wasn't real. Just two people in a confined space who had gotten tangled together in their sleep.

It wasn't real.

Carefully, Rachel detangled from the man. Dane didn't wake up, so she retreated to the bathroom. Sunlight peeked around the blinds. Rachel sighed.

Now it was time to get back to their reality.

One where she'd hopefully come up with a new lead.

Suzy's personal shopper/head of security had done it again. Rachel slid comfortably into a pair of blue jeans and a long-sleeved blouse. Both were flattering but sensible. Really, she had half a mind to ask Suzy for the man's information when this was all over.

Rachel hurried through brushing her teeth, washing her face and rebraiding her hair before going back into the bedroom. To her surprise, Dane was awake and sitting on the edge of the bed. His head was bent over his phone.

"Anything new happen while we were sleeping?" she ventured, trying to keep the burn of a blush from crawling up her neck. Just thinking about how warm the man had been against her was toeing the line of keeping her cool and becoming obviously distracted.

"No. Everyone is still following leads." He cursed then apologized. "I was hoping sleep might help but—"

Rachel clapped her hands, cutting him off. Before she'd lost her mental footing by waking in Dane's arms, she had been on to something.

"It did," she exclaimed. "At least, I think it did. The man from yesterday who still hasn't been identified—Knife Guy? Right before Overalls showed up, when he was talking to Tucker, he mentioned that Tucker buckled under pressure. Especially at—"

Dane's eyes widened.

"Every football game," he finished. He jumped up, closed the gap between them in one fluid motion and picked Rachel up. She gave a surprised laugh as he spun her around, put her down and kissed her on the cheek. "They went to school together *and* played on the same football team. You're brilliant!" He dialed a number and was in the next room talking to whoever was on the receiving end in a flash.

Rachel touched her cheek.

It was a good thing Dane couldn't see her.

She had no doubt she was as red as a cherry.

CHANCE SHOWED UP just after lunch. The rest of the department was spread thin, and if Dane was being honest, he preferred working with the freelancing cowboy. At least, when he wanted to do something that Billy and his friends might shoot down. Chance rarely said no. He was more of a "how can we minimize the damage?" kind of guy.

Not that Dane believed their plan was all that dangerous.

"We checked every place we could think of online to see if we could pull up a yearbook of Tucker's graduating class," he explained again. "Nothing from that year has been digitized that we can tell and the principal was less than helpful over the phone."

"We also looked through the social media accounts of people graduating around the same time to see if they posted any throwback pictures, but came up short," Rachel added. "Tucker isn't that much older than us, but for whatever reason, finding even a candid photo from his class has been hard."

"We did find one picture of the football team from the same year, but it's from a newspaper and you can't make out many of the faces. Plus, no names."

Chance nodded between them. "So we're taking a field trip to…?"

Dane passed him a piece of paper with an address on it.

"Kipsy South Academy," he answered.

Chance whistled low.

"Not a cheap school back in the day," he said. "Heck, not even now for that matter."

"Which is probably why the principal is giving us a hard time over the phone," Rachel pointed out.

Chance looked between them.

"Okay, you've got me sold," he declared. Chance thumbed back at the front of the cabin. "I switched to an associate's SUV so we can all fit. How long a trip is it?"

Dane and Rachel had already plotted the route out. The private school wasn't familiar to Dane, but he'd been there once before. "Forty-five minutes give or take."

Chance tipped his hat down. "Add a half hour of making sure no one is following us and we're square."

Dane smirked. "You sure you aren't interested in joining the department? You'd definitely fit in."

Chance waved him off. "You couldn't pay me enough to be stuck inside as long as you all are. Plus, I aim to never be pinned down." The cowboy sent a wink to Rachel. "I'm what you might call a rolling stone."

Dane rolled his eyes, but not in annoyance. He was grateful Chance had offered to take them to the school. Not only that, but act as backup. He had a gun permit, was a solid shot and had a good head on his shoulders. Plus, he was quick with his reflexes. When a situation turned on its head, he reacted swiftly and kept his cool. He was the only reason Dane had agreed to let Rachel come along, too. The last time they'd been ambushed, he was outnumbered. Even though Dane had killed the man they would *hopefully* find out more about, he liked having another gun on his side.

The drive to Kipsy South Academy was uneventful. Rachel used Dane's burner to call and check on Lonnie, while Dane and Chance reviewed the case. Again. He was starting to feel like Rachel had the night before. So many questions he felt like he was constantly on the brink of a headache.

"I think the lady should do the talking," Chance said. He parked in the private school's side parking lot and cut the engine. Kipsy might be a big city, but its private school was on the small side.

"It's easier to catch flies with honey," Dane said.

Rachel seemed to agree. "I don't know much about this school, but I have heard about the man who runs it. Gerald Boyle is what one of the PTA moms at Darby Middle calls a man with a Napoleon complex, especially when it comes to being around other men." She gave them a wry smile. "Translation, don't try to assert any dominance, or not even my assurances that he's important will land."

Dane raised his eyebrow at that. It earned a deeper smirk from the woman. She leaned closer. "You're wondering if I have ever done that to you, aren't you?"

She winked. Chance laughed.

Apparently, Dane wasn't the only one starting to get excited at the prospect of a new lead.

Gerald Boyle was a short, stocky man in his early sixties. He wore a full suit and abruptly made it clear he wasn't fond of Dane. The PTA mom and Rachel had been right on the money. He'd started talking about them needing a warrant. Around that time Rachel had steered the man into his office, honey in her voice. Minutes later and they were laughing. He led them to a classroom in the back of the school. It belonged to the yearbook students and had a closet filled with at least one copy of each year since the school had opened in the seventies.

"Take your time," Gerald said, attention on Rachel only. "And let me know if you need anything."

Rachel said thank you, smiling for all she was worth.

When Gerald had gone, Dane couldn't help himself. "Fly, meet Honey," he whispered.

Rachel laughed. Then it was down to business. Chance stayed by the empty classroom's closed door, just in case, while Dane and Rachel divided and conquered searching for the yearbook in question. It took longer than he would have liked, but finally Rachel clapped her hands and pointed to the leather-bound book.

"Here's hoping Tucker and his friend weren't talking about playing football in middle school instead," she said.

The mood in the classroom changed as they flipped through the book to the football team spreads. Dane scanned the group picture, but it was too small to really tell many of the players apart.

"At least we know he was on the team for sure," Rachel said when he went to the next page. She pointed to the individual picture of Tucker. Even now Dane felt some residual anger for the man. He turned to the next page, not recognizing the man who had attacked Rachel. "Oh, look! There's Knife—"

Rachel stopped midsentence. Even out of his periphery, Dane saw her tense. He was a second from asking what was wrong when he saw two things. Or, rather, two *people*.

The first was indeed the man from the day before. Younger but with a smile that caused anger to erupt in Dane all over again, the teen staring back at them was Wyatt Hall. Their Knife Guy. A man Dane had felt no guilt about stopping before he could hurt Rachel anymore.

However, it was the teen's portrait *next* to Wyatt's that had stalled Dane out.

"What's wrong?" Chance asked, concern lacing his tone. He strode over, cowboy hat in hand. "Did you find him?"

Dane was the first to recover.

He nodded.

"His name is Wyatt Hall," he answered, phone already out.

"Then what's the problem? What's got you two stiff as boards?"

Dane didn't look at Rachel's expression, but not because he was worried what it showed. Instead he was worried what he looked like. He'd gone from trying to solve their present to *slam bam*, back in the past. Still, he answered. "The boy next to Wyatt is Marcus the Martyr." Apparently named Marcus Highland, something the department had never been able to figure out. "The leader of the Saviors of the South."

Chance whistled again.

"So Tucker, Wyatt and Marcus all knew each other when they were teens," he reiterated. "How much do you want to bet this Levi guy is in here, too?"

Chance took over searching through the yearbook. Dane texted Billy and Detective Foster Wyatt's name. Rachel remained quiet.

"Well, he wasn't listed in the football roster but—" Chance waved Dane back over. He pointed to a single class photo. The name Levi Turner was listed underneath it. "It's either a series of incredibly relevant coincidences or—how much you want to bet—this Levi is the same man tangled up with Tucker and the late Marcus and Wyatt."

"You think Tucker and Levi want revenge for Marcus's death? And that's what this is all about?" Dane ventured. It had been seven years since Marcus had been taken down by a SWAT sharpshooter on loan from the next county over. Exacting revenge now for their friend would be an interesting move. One that didn't make sense, especially when Lonnie was involved.

"I've seen men and women do crazy things," Chance said, picking up on his thoughts. "The reasoning behind waiting years before avenging a friend can boil down to a lot. Maybe they had to bide their time until they got the funds or the plan in place. Maybe they tried before and something went wrong. Heck, maybe Tucker decided he didn't want to be a part of whatever it was and tried to hide from Wyatt and Levi, but they found him now anyways."

"That could be why he tried to run," Dane conceded. Though it didn't feel right. Why not take Lonnie with him if he was bailing? And why did the men want Lonnie to begin with? Unless it was to use him for leverage against his uncle. Yet Wyatt had talked about keeping the boy safe.

It still wasn't adding up.

Dane was going to say as much when Rachel finally spoke. Her voice was even, calm.

"Maybe we're missing a key piece of the puzzle." She turned and met Dane's gaze. Sweet blues pulled him in. "And, maybe, Marcus isn't dead at all."

Chapter Fifteen

Chance left Rachel and Dane at the cabin like a dog
homed in on a new scent. In the time it took her to
watch the cowboy drive off, Dane wasn't that far
behind. He set up shop at a small dining table with
his laptop and phone. Rachel watched as he worked,
calling what seemed to be an endless list of contacts,
trying to make sense of the connection between Marcus, Levi, Wyatt and Tucker.

And also trying to track down Marcus's body.

Neither man had fought hard against Rachel's theory that the leader of the Saviors could still be alive.
She'd fully expected pushback. Yet Chance had surprised her.

"The thought had crossed my mind," he had admitted. Then he'd shared a look with Dane that was
loaded. One neither elaborated on out loud. On the
way back to the cabin, they'd sidestepped the possibility to talk about slightly more plausible reasons
why Tucker would do what he had done.

They'd also switched over to the broadcast, wondering if it was Levi's voice filling the car.

Rachel held back while Dane continued to thrive in his element. She picked a random book off the bookshelf and flipped through its pages, but the words blurred every time she tried to focus. What if she was right? What if Marcus was alive? What if the man who had killed her husband was still causing chaos?

What if he was after Dane now?

Rachel's heart squeezed at the thought. Then she was angry. She fisted her hand against the love seat. One person shouldn't be allowed to take so much from another.

It just wasn't right.

Rachel sighed into the open book. Her emotions were all over the place. She needed a distraction. She needed a reprieve from her own mental torture.

"I need wine," she announced.

Dane looked up from his laptop, eyebrow cocked. Rachel jumped off the love seat and headed to the pantry without a follow-up. The small closet had cookies, chips, pasta, pancake mix, cereal and two boxes of fruit snacks. Surely, Suzy had added wine to the obscure list. Rachel continued to go through the kitchen when the pantry search proved fruitless. Dane watched her but kept quiet. Which was good; she was two seconds from picking a fight out of frustration.

"Eureka!"

Above the refrigerator was a lone bottle of Prosecco. There were even a couple of wineglasses.

"Do you think that's a good idea?" Dane had the gall to ask. Rachel ignored him until she found a corkscrew.

"What I think is that, as long as we're here, I can't do much to help," she said. The cork came out easily enough. "Other than do what we already have been doing, which is asking a whole lot of questions. Since I've already asked about all the ones I can think of, that leaves me thinking about either being chased by two men, having one almost shoot me the next day, seeing *his* dead body or…" She paused to fill her glass, then continued. "Or my least favorite, thinking that the man behind it all might just be the man who killed my husband."

She turned around, full glass in hand, and tried to ignore the invisible walls she knew had risen around the man. "So, I think the best route for me to take at this particular juncture is to sit on that love seat, try to read whatever book that is, drink that Prosecco we were lucky enough to find, and try to pretend that I don't feel as helpless as I did seven years ago when that son of a bitch Marcus Highland decided he needed to make a statement."

Rachel didn't wait for a response. She was close to tears, angrier than she thought she had been. She settled back in her spot on the love seat and took her first sip of the wine.

Dane, bless his heart, did the right thing.

He didn't say a word.

THE WINE WASN'T a bad idea, but it wasn't a good one, either.

Dane kept quiet as Rachel followed through on her plan for the next few hours. She sat on the love seat, drank her wine and read through a book about a city girl moving to a small town. In that time the acute worry of Marcus and his merry men dulled. The frustration and anxiousness were replaced by a warmth. Dane took calls outside or typed along his keyboard while the day crawled by. For a little while, Rachel forgot about their problems.

But then the city girl in her book ran into a problem that transcended the pages between Rachel's hands.

"You left me," he said. "Without a word, you got on a bus and came to this hick town. Why?"

Even though it was nothing more than a book and the situation was nowhere near the same, something in Rachel snapped. Helped, no doubt, by the wine she had once thought would work as a distraction. She put the book down, took a deep breath and finally asked the question she had avoided asking for years.

"Why did you leave me?"

DANE OPENED HIS mouth to say *something*, but Rachel kept on.

"And don't you deny that's exactly what happened," she said, voice rising as she stood. "One day you were there and then one day you weren't. Then you started avoiding me and, eventually, I gave up trying to connect. I gave up trying to *fix* whatever it was that had broken. I *let it go*. But now? After everything we've just been through? All I want to know now is *why*. Why did you leave, Dane? I want to know. I think I deserve that much."

Pretending he didn't know the woman a few feet from him well would have been a lie. Before David had died, Dane had already been friends with the woman, able to be around her with enjoyment and ease. After David passed, that friendship had only grown stronger, weaving together with something else in common. Tragedy. They'd become closer.

Too close.

That was how Dane knew that Rachel had reached the end of her grace toward him. Her eyes were shining, her body was rigid. Even from the distance between them, he saw her teeth gritting together after she finished talking. She was angry. She was hurt. She was looking for an answer.

One Dane still couldn't give.

Not after the way the case had possibly turned back toward the past.

So Dane took the easy way out and felt the fool for it.

"It was the guilt," he said simply. Not entirely a lie, not entirely the truth. "The anniversary of David's death was coming up and there I was, eating dinner with you. Talking. Laughing. It was too much." He shook his head slowly. "Being around you was too much."

The hurt was immediate. Rachel's whole body was seemingly affected by the sting of his words. Dane hated it. More than anything he'd always wanted to protect her from any and all pain. Yet there he was. The cause of it.

Rachel dropped her gaze and walked to the bedroom door. Dane watched her go, refusing to follow. It wouldn't do either of them any good.

"You know," Rachel started to say, pausing in the doorway and turning to face him again, "when you told me David died because of *your* plan, I was angry. But, like I've said before, never for one moment was I angry at you. Do you want to know why that is, Dane?"

It was his turn to become rigid. He didn't answer. He didn't think she expected him to, either.

"Because a man named Marcus was the one who killed my husband. *Our* best friend. While all you did was try your damnedest to save him. I was proud of you for that then and I'm still proud of it now. So whatever hang-ups or guilt trips you want to continue to feed, don't put any of that on me. I never forgave you, Dane, because I never blamed you."

And then she was gone.

RACHEL LOOKED UP at the ceiling and let her eyes adjust to the darkness. She'd been asleep, but for how long? A dim light filtered in from beneath the bedroom door. The spot next to her in bed was empty and cold. Not that she expected Dane to be there. She'd finally let him know that his abrupt abandonment and following absence through the years had left their marks.

Rachel sighed into the silence.

Now she finally knew why he'd done both and she didn't know how to process it. She had meant what she said, though. She didn't want the man spending any more of his days blaming himself and using her as an excuse to do it. Rachel wasn't going to have that, but at the same time, she didn't know how to make *Dane* accept that.

I guess that's not up to me, she thought. An ache of loss echoed in her chest at the sentiment.

Rachel rolled over and looked at the digital readout on her cell phone's screen. Not only had she retreated to the bedroom before she could *really* lose it earlier, but she'd managed to take a nap that had stretched well into the night. The emotional toll had been draining; the wine hadn't helped.

That same wine was making her feel the need to drink some water. She sighed, swung her legs over the side of the bed, and padded to the bathroom with her pajamas in tow. She had been so upset earlier that she hadn't changed out of her clothes. She had just wanted to close her eyes. Now she was better. She washed her face, brushed her teeth and nodded to her reflection in the mirror.

She wasn't proud that she had gotten tipsy and yelled at Dane, but it had been a long time coming. Now all they could do was move past it.

Rachel's stomach dropped.

How Dane had moved past it before was to cut her completely out of his life. After the case was solved, would he do that again?

Rachel felt like she was constantly sighing, but there another one was as she crawled back into bed. She wasn't tired anymore, but that didn't mean she was about to go get into Dane's personal space. Especially since he had admitted being around her was "too much."

Rachel felt another sigh about to escape when a knock on the door distracted it. She reached over to the bedside lamp and clicked it on.

"Come in," she called.

Dark eyes swept across the room and landed on her.

"I heard you moving around," he greeted. "I… Well…"

He rubbed a hand across the back of his neck. The movement made his biceps jump. Rachel tried to ignore it.

"Spit it out," Rachel said, surprised at how brash the command sounded. Still, it did the trick.

"I tried to sleep on the couch, and if there's one thing I'm certain about the two of us, it's that we're tall people." He managed to look sheepish. "I was wondering if, well… I know you're mad at me, but— Well, I—"

Rachel rolled her eyes and patted the bed next to her. "You can still sleep in here, Dane. I'm not going to kick you out."

Dane chanced a small smile. It, plus the promise of him being so close to her again, made Rachel's heartbeat start to speed up. It was annoying. Dane had hurt her, and just because she wasn't going to make him sleep on the floor, that didn't mean she couldn't stay grumpy. To prove this point to them both without saying a word, she turned the light off and rolled over, her back to the rest of the room.

Dane was smart not to comment. He moved around the bedroom and bathroom until she felt the bed dip beneath his weight. She tensed, making sure to not slide toward him. She just hoped her body stayed as vigilant while she was asleep. Waking up in Dane's arms after their short but brutal conversation wouldn't be ideal.

A few minutes went by without a word. The silence was almost too loud. Rachel waited for his breathing to even out to let her know he had fallen asleep, although after a few more minutes passed, it remained the same. She had half a mind to roll over and peek. But what would that solve?

"You awake?"

Rachel opened her eyes in a flash, worried for the briefest of moments that Dane had somehow heard her thoughts. She stared at the wall, trying to tamp down the spike in her adrenaline at his words.

"I am," she said after a moment. "What's u—?"

"It was your yellow dress. The one with daisies on it." His voice had fallen into an even lower than normal baritone. "We were supposed to meet for lunch and try out the new Italian place on Main Street. I'd already been in Darby that morning to talk to the chief, so I decided to stretch my legs and walk the park across from the post office. It being a nice day outside didn't hurt."

Slowly, Rachel rolled over to face him. He was lying on his back, staring up at the ceiling. She dared not speak.

"So I parked next to the post office and walked to the fountain," he continued. "There was some yoga class going on and I didn't want to seem like I was creeping, so I kept walking until I got to the other side of the park."

Even in the dim light from beneath the bathroom door, Rachel saw the man smile. "Then there you were. Across the road, parked outside Sadie's Bookstore, angry as a kicked hornet's nest. Your tire was flat, but by God, that wasn't stopping you. You already had the car jacked up and the bolts off the hubcaps. I instantly wanted to help you, which instantly made me laugh. I knew just about what you'd say if I tried to take over. 'I've done this enough times to know I can change this tire faster than you, Dane Jones.' After that you'd probably count off all the times you'd changed a tire since your mom had taught you how to do it when you were in high school." His smile smoothed out. Rachel nearly held her breath.

"And then I was looking at that dress, the one with the daisies," he said. "I'd never seen it before. I was sure I'd remember it if I had." Dane turned his head to meet her gaze. "That's when I realized I was in love with you. And *that's* why I had to leave."

Chapter Sixteen

The entire cast from *Game of Thrones* could have walked into the bedroom right then and Rachel wouldn't have even batted an eye. The moment Dane finished his declaration, all Rachel could do was stare.

"I should have told you," he said. "Instead of just going, but—"

Rachel's mind took a back seat as her body went into overdrive. She closed the space between them with little effort and pressed her lips to his with little thought.

Dane's reaction time was slow, but Rachel didn't care.

She needed to kiss him. She needed to touch him. She needed to let out some of the energy that had ignited within her at his revelation.

Because Dane saying he loved her hadn't irrevocably changed her. No. What he'd said was better.

Because, Rachel realized, she didn't just want to be friends with the man next to her.

She wanted more.

Much more.

And apparently Dane still did, too.

He answered her kiss with force, pushing his lips against hers with a notable hunger. He rolled onto his side, deepening the kiss with a swipe of his tongue. Rachel responded with her own exploration. Even at the odd angle, Dane threaded one hand into her hair. He was gentle with it, yet she still gasped against him.

His body tensed as he broke the kiss.

Dark eyes she had missed more than she had realized searched her face.

"Are you oka—?" he started, voice husky and raw.

Rachel didn't let him finish the question.

She was back to his lips and, like on the night before, she entered his embrace. The hand in her hair fastened her mouth to his while his other hand grabbed and pulled her hips closer. Rachel didn't waste any time showing she wanted more than his lips. She fingered the hem of his shirt and then slid her hands up and underneath it. They explored the hard surface of his stomach and abs. His bare skin electric beneath her own.

Dane made a guttural noise deep in his throat.

It was more than encouraging.

Rachel tugged up on the fabric of the shirt until

Dane got the hint. He broke their kiss long enough to pull his shirt off. It was thrown across the room and out of sight. Rachel decided to join in. Or at least she tried.

Dane had other ideas.

He rolled over until he was straddling her and then bent over and worked the buttons of her pajama top. The task of getting her out of her shirt could have gone a lot faster, but apparently he was going for extra credit. Starting at her collarbone, Dane pressed his lips to her skin. The contact was dazzling and only became more pronounced the lower his lips traveled. With each new unfastened button, there was Dane. Trailing his lips and tongue down her newly bare skin. When there was nothing left to unbutton, Dane pulled her up and against him as she shimmied out of the top.

There was a moment when they sat there, bare chests pressed together, hearts beating, breathing, moving against each other, when Rachel felt like they were at some kind of precipice. An important one.

"You said you *were* in love with me," she whispered, breathless. "Are you still?"

Dane ran his hand across her cheek and tucked a strand of hair behind her ear. In the dim light she could see his smile.

"I never stopped."

Then his mouth was over hers and he was pushing her back on the bed. The rest of their clothes disappeared as their bodies, and hearts, finally intertwined.

DANE OPENED HIS eyes and felt the warmth of the woman he'd loved for years tucked safely within his arms. It was like a weight had been lifted from his entire body as he looked at Rachel's sleeping form. He'd finally told her the truth. The full reason he'd put distance between them.

In the year following David's death, he'd gone from being a friend to falling in love with her. Dane didn't know when it had happened or how—he definitely hadn't been looking for it—but there it was. He was in love with his best friend's girl.

David had once joked that if anything ever happened to him in the line of duty, Dane should look out for Rachel. Dane could bet he hadn't meant to fall in love with her a few weeks after the anniversary of his death.

An ache of guilt pushed through him at the thought.

It was like Rachel could sense his turmoil. She stirred in his arms. He pasted on a smile.

"Good morning," he greeted, eyeing the readout on her phone. It was just after seven. "Sorry if I woke you."

Rachel stretched her legs and arms out, her body vibrating against his. The movement plus the absolutely naked smoothness of her skin was jarring. Not in any unpleasant way, just not on the same wavelength as the guilt settled in his stomach. Having Rachel so close and in such a vulnerable position was teasing his more primal urges. He tried to focus.

"No, it's fine," she said, rolling onto her back to look at him. "I wanted to get up early today anyways." She smiled and then put a hand in front of her mouth. "But if you'll excuse me and my morning breath for a moment."

Dane laughed as the woman wasted no time in escaping from beneath the sheets. She grabbed his discarded shirt, threw it on, and sent him a quick wink before disappearing into the bathroom. He didn't like the empty spot next to him. However they weren't on vacation. He had a job to do and bad men to catch. Not lie around in bed, tormenting himself over a woman with denim-blue eyes and a set of lips that rocked his world.

No, he needed to focus.

He swiped his phone off the nightstand. No new texts or emails. No new calls.

Trying to exhume Marcus's body was a waiting game. One that couldn't be finished until a judge approved the request. Billy was going to work on that as soon as Judge Deal got to his office. Once they knew for certain one way or the other that his body was what had been buried under a single-named headstone in one of Kipsy's cemeteries, the lead on him, plus the men from the past few days, had hit a road block. At least, for Dane it had.

Finding Knife Guy, aka Wyatt, and Levi in the yearbook had been exciting. Yet that excitement had ebbed as the night before dragged on. Neither man was in the sheriff department's database and neither had a social media presence to follow. Everywhere Dane and the department had looked seemed to be a dead end.

It was like none of the men existed past their names and pictures in one edition of the Kipsy South Academy yearbook.

Which meant either they were really good at hiding their trails or they had the resources to help them keep themselves under wraps.

Or both.

There was also still the question of how Lonnie fit into everything.

Why did Levi want him?

What did Tucker know about it all?

Dane scrubbed a hand down his face. He could feel a headache start to form behind his eyes while the stress in his shoulders became heavier. It was hard to focus on a case that had so many questions but no answers. He rolled his shoulders back, trying to ease the building tension. What he really needed to do was to hit the gym. Work out some of the stress. Try to get his body and mind on the same page again.

The shower came on in the next room. Dane put his phone down as Rachel opened the door. She wasn't wearing his shirt anymore.

"I'm going to take a quick shower," she said conversationally. "I was wondering if you wanted to join me."

Dane couldn't help smirking.

His body and mind certainly seemed to get on the same page fast at that.

CHANCE SHOWED UP at lunch. He barely made it into the cabin before his hat was off and he was launching into a story.

"I was trying to figure out where Tucker went when he left the house the other night," he summarized for them, perching on the edge of the couch. "But I was coming up empty. So I decided to ask some different questions like who the hell this man is. If you know enough about a person, it's not hard to guess where he might go or do in any given situation. So, *who is Tucker Hughes*?"

Rachel didn't know if the cowboy wanted an answer, but *she* sure wanted one. "Who is he?"

Chance slapped his knee and snapped his fingers, excitement clear in his eyes. "He's a quiet man who has spent his life staying out of people's ways. He graduated from high school, got a manual labor job in construction, and has spent the past few decades maintaining a quiet existence." A wicked grin pulled up the corner of his mouth. "And, according to a high school sweetheart I managed to track down thanks to the yearbook, he's also an only child."

"Wait, what?" Rachel asked.

"He's raising his nephew," Dane pointed out. "I

might be an only child, but I know you need a sibling to have one of those."

Chance put up his hands to stop them from continuing.

"Listen, believe me, I barked up that tree when she said that," he said. "But she said she was one-hundred-percent certain that he was a single child. So, without seeming like I was calling her a liar, I asked if she could direct me to anyone else who was friends with him back in the day. She said he was a total loner and he only hung out with her and one other person while they were in high school." The grin grew. "And that person was none other than Marcus Highland."

Rachel straightened her back. She felt her nostrils flare. She never would get used to hearing that name. Dane had a similar reaction but then was typing away at his laptop. Rachel couldn't see what he was looking up. She turned back to Chance.

"So what are you thinking?" she had to ask. "And what about Lonnie?"

Chance was practically beaming.

"I'm thinking that Tucker doesn't have a brother, but Marcus Highland does," he said. "Or did."

The cowboy turned his attention to his friend. Dane's brows were knitted together, his eyes narrowed and scanning the screen. Whatever he had been looking for was right in front of him. Chance must have sensed that, too. He waited until Dane caught on to his unsaid thought.

"Almost eleven years ago a John Highland was killed in his prison cell by a fellow inmate," Dane said, still reading the information on his computer screen. "He was there for felony drug possession, although his wife claimed the arresting deputy had planted the drugs. She tried to sue the department. The Riker County Sheriff's Department." He paused to finish reading. "She passed away in a car accident before it could go anywhere." Dane finally looked up. He only had eyes for her. "Leaving behind one child. A baby boy."

Chance nodded. "Now, I can't say for certain if John Highland is really related to Marcus, especially since we can't seem to find any trace of Marcus other than that yearbook, but when I went to look into what happened to that baby boy…well, I came up empty." Chance shrugged. Then he leaned closer. "But guess when Lonnie started showing up in Tucker's life?"

Rachel shook her head.

"No way," she breathed. "It can't be."

Chance nodded. "Two months after Jasmine Highland's death, Tucker Hughes became the legal guardian of Lonnie."

Rachel shook her head again, trying to come up with another explanation.

"That can't be," she challenged. "You can't just say you're related to some kid and take him in when it's not true."

"With the right papers, the right amount of money, and the wrong people, you can do just about anything."

Rachel had opened her mouth to try to attack that thought when Dane spoke up.

"Wyatt said Tucker was supposed to keep the boy safe," he said. "That's why. Marcus wasn't just coming for Lonnie for some kind of ransom or leverage to use. He was coming for him because Lonnie is *his* nephew. Not Tucker's." Dane fisted his hand against the tabletop. "And if this is all true, that's why Marcus was so hell-bent on the idea of corruption in the department back then." His expression softened. "And why he might have targeted a prison transport van to help make his statement."

Rachel's head felt like it was going to explode. "But why? Why do *all* this? Why not just raise his nephew himself? Why come for him now?" She threw her hands in the air. "I still don't understand!"

The sound of a phone vibrating made them all turn to the tabletop.

"It's Billy," Dane said. He scooped up the phone and answered it. Billy didn't say much, but it was enough. "I'm on my way."

Dane was standing taller when he hung up.

"I think it's about time we get some answers," he said. "And I think it's time to get some from Tucker himself. He just woke up and is ready to talk."

Chapter Seventeen

Rachel picked at the invisible lint on her jeans. Dane put his hand over hers to settle it but kept his gaze straight ahead. She took a deep breath and glanced around the small waiting room.

Chance was leaning against the wall, hat in his hands and eyes closed. Two local officers originally tasked with keeping a watch over Tucker were talking among themselves just outside the doorway. Detective Foster was pacing through the back of the room, head bent over his phone. Occasionally he would make a call, sometimes he would pull Dane over to talk to him.

Breaking out the theory that Tucker Hughes had adopted Marcus Highland's nephew had given the department a new direction to look into. It had also given the sheriff enough ammo to convince the judge that exhuming Marcus's body was the right call to make. Illegally adopting Lonnie was one thing. Illegally adopting Lonnie to keep the boy safe while Marcus continued to do devious things was another.

Rachel let out a breath, frustrated.

"Should Lonnie be in there right now?" she asked for what felt like the umpteenth time.

"We can't prove Tucker isn't Lonnie's legal guardian right now," he reiterated. "Even if we could, Lonnie has been with that man since he was a toddler. He wanted to see him."

"Tucker tried to leave him," Rachel muttered. Dane squeezed her hand.

"Don't worry. Suzy is in there with him," he reassured her. "She'll make sure Tucker doesn't say anything that could hurt Lonnie."

Rachel knew he was right, but still her nerves weren't happy. It was nice to have a theory that might get them answers to what was going on, but it was a theory she wasn't excited to entertain. Marcus had been shot and buried by the state. When no one could figure out his true identity, all he'd gotten was his first name and the date he died on his tombstone. The same date that was on David's, too.

What if he *was* still alive?

What had he been doing the past several years?

What was the endgame?

Dane ran his thumb across her wrist.

"I know," he whispered soothingly. "I know."

Rachel took a deep breath and then let it out, trying to rein in the excess anxiety making her feel even more crazy in their current situation. As much as he hated it, Dane had told her the truth during the ride over.

Right now was a waiting game. One the entire department was playing. Everyone had a part they were looking into.

"Once we get that first answer, the rest will fall in line like dominoes," Dane had said.

Rachel understood his confidence. He trusted the men and women in the department with more than just the case. He trusted them with his life. It was nice to know that, while Dane had left his original life plan after David's passing, he had still found his place in the world. One that included a job he loved and coworkers who were more like family. It was just nice to know he hadn't been alone for the past few years.

"Here we go."

Rachel looked up as Suzy rounded the corner, Lonnie at her side. Dane and Rachel stood. Chance started over. Suzy smiled and motioned to the drink vending machine in the corner. She handed the boy two dollars.

"Like I promised," she said with a grin.

Lonnie took the money and was off. It gave Suzy time to talk to them.

"Tucker is on some painkillers, so he isn't one-hundred percent there, if you ask me." She dove in. "But he knows where he is and what happened. I think he also is very aware that we know he left Lonnie. He looked nervous and guilty more than anything else."

"What did he say to Lonnie?" Rachel asked.

Suzy rubbed her stomach. Her expression hardened.

"Not enough, if you ask me," she said. "Lonnie did most of the talking. Told him what happened in the house the other day." Suzy looked directly at Rachel. "Talked a lot about you. Said you would die before letting him sacrifice himself to the man who was downstairs. Then he talked about your wound and how it looked under the bandage."

Rachel touched her wrist and smiled for a moment at the boy's earlier curiosity to see it.

Then Suzy turned to Dane. She lowered her voice. "I don't know how their relationship was before this all happened, but I don't think they're all that close. Lonnie didn't even try to hug him. Just kind of patted the bed. Tucker didn't try anything, either. It was almost like they were strangers."

"The rumor at school is that Tucker views Lonnie as more of an obligation than family," Rachel said, matching Suzy's low tone.

"Which is in line with our new theory," Chance added. "He might actually be an obligation for Tucker." Rachel narrowed her eyes at the cowboy. He held up his hand and defended himself. "You know what I mean."

Rachel glanced over at the boy. Her heart squeezed at the thought of him living with a man who viewed him as some kind of job or chore.

"Can we go see Tucker now?" Dane asked. His voice was tight. He was trying to stay professional, but Rachel heard the anger beneath his words. "I'd really like to ask that man some questions."

Suzy nodded. "My advice? Don't press him too hard too fast," she said. "I don't like to make snap judgments about people I don't know, but honestly, I think he's one heck of a coward. You might break him before you get what you want."

Dane muttered some not-nice words. Rachel touched his arm.

"I want to stay out here with Lonnie," she told him. "I don't want to see that man yet. I don't have professional training in keeping my opinions to myself."

"I'm sure Lonnie would like that," Dane said with a small smile. "He seems to be a fan."

"While you all do that, I'm going to go call Billy and see how things are going with him," Suzy added. She looked over their shoulder to Detective Foster. "Then see what Caleb has going on. Deputy Mills is supposed to be on his way here soon to talk."

Rachel once again pictured each of the people around her with one piece of the puzzle. The anxiety of waiting settled back onto her shoulders. She would be happy when this was all over.

Dane and Chance disappeared down the hallway while Suzy went in the opposite direction. Rachel walked over to the vending machine in time to see Lonnie scowling at it.

"What did that machine ever do to you?" Rachel teased.

Lonnie looked over and let out a loud, long sigh.

"I wanted a Pepsi," he said. "This one doesn't have any. This week has sucked."

Rachel was going to correct him but decided to agree. "It *has* sucked, hasn't it?"

Lonnie looked surprised. Rachel snorted. It made him smile.

"Yeah, it has," he said, enthused. "They even brought me homework to do yesterday. But I told them I was too emotional."

His smile turned into a grin.

Rachel couldn't help laughing.

Despite everything, the boy had a sense of humor. It was endearing.

"Here, why don't we go look at the vending machines down the hall?" Rachel suggested. "See if they don't have a Pepsi or two. Maybe some candy while we're at it."

Lonnie nodded, eyes lighting up. He followed as she went to the two police officers watching the area.

"We're going to go to the vending machines down there," she said, pointing down the hall. They could see half of one of the machines just from where they were standing. It was probably the only reason they allowed them to go. Rachel turned to Detective Foster. His face was pinched, his attention narrowed. Whatever news he was getting over the phone was probably just as frustrating as all the other news they'd already gotten.

"So, do you like the place you're staying at?" Rachel asked as they meandered along the hall. She decided to avoid asking the questions she wanted to, like how he was doing and if Tucker had ever talked about *not* being his uncle.

"It's okay," he said with a shrug. "There's a pool in the back, but they said it was better to stay inside even though I told them I'm really awesome at swimming."

She didn't miss how his chest seemed to swell with pride.

"Tucker doesn't like the water, but I do. I taught myself to swim when I was in third grade. I'm really fast."

"That's impressive. I can swim but not fast. I'm really good at floating, though." They came to a stop at the first of three vending machines. Rachel smiled as she spied one had Pepsi. A man was standing in front of it, looking for money in his pockets. "And you know, I really like water, too. I even have a creek next to my house."

"Really?" Lonnie asked.

"Yep. It's *just* deep enough to swim in but not *too* deep. But my favorite part is listening to it from the deck. It's really nice in the summer."

That seemed to impress Lonnie. He opened his mouth to say something when the man next to them spoke instead.

"It really *is* a lovely feature."

He turned around so fast that Rachel didn't think to feel threatened. She figured it was just a man trying to make conversation. But then he kept talking.

"If you make any move or try to alert those cops down the hall, Marnie is as good as dead."

Rachel felt her eyes widen.

"And that means looking at me in fear."

Rachel adjusted her expression. She fought the urge to look back toward the police officers. All she had to do was yell and they'd come. Or run back to them.

But he'd said Marnie's name.

"What do you mean Marnie's as good as dead?" Rachel did the math in her head quickly. The last time she had talked to the young woman had been the day of the broadcast. While a deputy was there, she'd gone into the house and gotten June the cat, promising to take care of her until things calmed down.

Guilt, strong and fast, bulldozed into Rachel's stomach.

With everything going on she hadn't thought about checking up on her friend. Or her cat for that matter. She should have, plain and simple.

"Oh, don't worry," the man said. "She and June are still alive. Just as long as you listen to me." He titled his gaze down to Lonnie. "As long as you *both* listen to me." He took a dollar bill out of his pocket and held it out to the boy. "You take this and put it in that first vending machine. I want you to pretend you're trying to decide on what to get, got it?"

Lonnie didn't hesitate. He nodded. Without looking at Rachel, he took a step back and in front of the right vending machine. It kept Lonnie in the sight line of the officers. Rachel, however, was just outside it.

"Now, Ms. Roberts, here's the deal," the man began. "You and Lonnie are going to come with us, but unlike the last two times, you *aren't* going to cause any trouble." He motioned behind him. Farther down the hall a man she hadn't seen until now pushed his coat aside long enough so she could see he was wearing a gun.

"That man is the only one in the world who knows the right thing to say to another one of my associates *not* here. If he doesn't say that right thing in the next five minutes, that other associate will start the process of bleeding out young Miss Marnie." He steepled his fingers in front of him. "Now, *that right thing* will only be said when you and the boy walk out with us without any fuss. And let me point out that this associate of mine really doesn't have a taste for you. Considering you're the reason his friend was killed."

"Wyatt," Rachel breathed.

The man arched his eyebrow, but he smiled.

"That's right," he confirmed. "Wyatt was his friend and he's more than ready to kill yours. So let's get this show on the road, all right?"

"You're just going to kill us all anyways," Rachel pointed out, sure of her words. "Our chances at survival go down exponentially if we go with you."

She believed what she said and she hoped Lonnie heard that confidence in her voice. She was saying it for his benefit, not hers. He'd already tried to sacrifice himself when Wyatt was around. At the same time, Rachel couldn't damn Marnie just yet.

"Oh, as much as I wish we could, that's not the plan." He glanced at Lonnie. "The boy is off limits. You are on the fence. And Marnie? Marnie is just good ol' bait." He grinned. "And not to be a broken record, but whether she lives or dies is up to you. It isn't our decision at all."

Rachel's stomach twisted. She pictured the first time she'd met sweet, innocent Marnie. Awkward, talkative, and completely indifferent when it came to personal space. Since then the young girl had grown into a wonderful young woman. Rachel pictured her days ago, worried that something had happened to Rachel and distraught at just the thought.

Rachel took a shuddering breath.

Her heart sank.

The man's eyes narrowed.

Forgive me, Marnie.

Rachel spun on her heel and pushed Lonnie as hard as she could farther into the sight line of the officers.

"Help!" she yelled at the top of her lungs.

Then, before either of the men could react, Rachel ran.

This time, it wasn't away from danger.

It was toward it.

Chapter Eighteen

Her head was nothing but a throbbing ache. Rachel opened her eyes and tenderly touched her cheek. It hurt, too. Her fingers were wet as she pulled them back.

What had happened?

Where was she?

It was dark. Cool but not too cold. She tried to let her eyes adjust as she reached out on either side of her. One hand touched something hard. The other went through air.

"Lonnie?"

Her voice fell flat in the darkness. Like she was somewhere tight. She waited, listening. No one responded, least of all Lonnie.

The hospital.

The men.

Rachel's heartbeat started to gallop.

She'd managed to tackle the man closest to them in the hospital hallway, but after that things got hazy. The throbbing of her head was a clue she couldn't ignore. She'd been hit in the head. Hard. Someone had knocked her out.

"Marnie?" she tried instead.

No response.

Rachel took a moment to take stock of herself. She wasn't tied up or bound. Her mouth wasn't covered, either. Aside from her head, there was no other pain. Still, slowly, she tested herself to see if there were any other limitations while also trying to figure out where she was.

She reached out to the spot where she'd connected with something hard and put her palm against it. Whatever it was, it was textured and firm. Rachel slid her hand up and then all the way to the floor. It was a wall. She put her palm against the floor and felt along it, hoping to find *something,* but came up short.

Rachel decided to follow that wall. She got up slowly and felt along it for a few steps before she hit another one. She did the same thing along the new wall until a foot or so later she hit another corner. Wherever she was, it was a very small room.

Alone in that very small, very dark, room.

Panic started to rise within her. Her breathing was becoming erratic. She traced the last wall back, hoping to find a door.

"Thank God," she whispered to herself. Her fingers wrapped around a doorknob. It turned but something caught when she pushed. Rachel turned the knob again and tried to push through. The door was blocked on the other side.

The panic in Rachel's chest quickly turned to fear.

"Help," she yelled, banging her fists against the door. "Help! Someone! I'm in here!"

Rachel beat at the door until the wound from her hand burned. She tried to open the door one last time. When it didn't move, she opened up her search perimeter. She moved along each of the walls again, this time with the intent of finding a light switch. When she came up empty, she moved backward, sweeping each foot out in an arc before she continued. Finally she felt something.

A string.

Rachel pulled it.

A fluorescent bulb came to life above her. She blinked against the new light. The room she was in *was* small. No windows, no furniture, just a cluster of boxes she was a few inches from tripping over near the middle. She turned back to the door and tried to open it again, as if seeing it would make some kind of difference. However, whatever was on the other side of it continued to resist.

Rachel turned her attention to the closest box. It was taped up. One name was written across its side in black Sharpie. The writing was familiar. So was the name.

"David," she read out loud.

Ice ran through her veins.

Slowly she looked around.

Rachel wasn't in a room. She was in a shed.

Her shed.

The one she had bought a few months back for behind her house. It had been too hot to move her excess boxes into it during the summer, so she'd only put in a few. The ones that were in there now were books. Rachel bent over and started to open the box closest to her. A book was better than nothing when it came to makeshift weapons.

A scraping sound made her turn. Movement shook the door. Rachel tried to claw the box open, needing to get her hands on *something*, but she ran out of time. A flood of light from outside came in.

Once again she blinked to get her bearings.

"Glad to see Levi didn't kill you."

A man filled the doorway. Tall, broad, and a mass of muscles. He had a shaved head and a nasty scar across his right forearm. A smaller but still angry scar puckered the skin at his neck. He wore a dark navy blazer and a matching pair of slacks. His shoes reflected sunlight. So did the long knife in his hand.

"You're Marcus Highland," Rachel said, voice stone. It wasn't a question. She'd seen his picture and she would never forget it. So he really wasn't dead.

Marcus nodded and stepped inside. He didn't shut the door, but the man from the hospital with the gun came into view. After he flashed her a smile and turned around. He was the guard. Beyond him Rachel could see the trees that separated her house and Marnie's property.

Marnie.

Rachel began to feel numb.

If she wasn't in the shed, then did that mean…?

"You know, I'm impressed with you," Marcus said. He stopped and leaned against the wall. Rachel backed up until her back hit the one opposite. He pointed the knife at her. Its blade glinted in the light. "You're craftier than I thought you would be. Here I thought you'd just freeze up when my friends came after you and Lonnie. Maybe fight back a little, run a little, too, but nothing like what you did at the school. It was a surprise to say the least. But it was also a bad plan. One my deceased partner Wyatt decided to attempt a little too early. But when Tucker said Lonnie had Saturday detention and *you* were the teacher in charge?" He shrugged. "I could see how he thought moving the timeline up was a good move. When two pieces line up like that? Well, it's hard to pass up the opportunity that arises from it."

He smiled. It sickened her.

"But I guess you taught Wyatt a lesson. Or should I say Captain Dane Jones did?" Marcus's eyes turned to slits for the briefest of moments. "Captain. I can't believe *he* made captain. I didn't think he'd have the stones."

The disgust that was clear in his voice made Rachel find her own.

"What's your plan?" she snapped. "Why do you want Lonnie now? Why come for him all these years later?"

Marcus didn't answer right away. Instead he studied her. It made her skin crawl, his brown eyes sweeping across her face like a machine trying to scan a code.

"You know," he finally said.

Rachel nodded.

"Lonnie is *your* nephew, not Tucker's," she confirmed. "But I don't understand why. You could have adopted him, but instead you started the Saviors of the South. Why? What was the point of it all? Why kill all those men?"

Rachel thought of David. Her voice broke enough to make her feel shame. She didn't want to give the man the satisfaction of her crying. The tears in her throat stayed down.

Marcus's expression stayed impassive. "Plans are hard to make and keep when corruption can take everyone and everything away from you."

"Your brother, John," Rachel stated. If Marcus was going to talk, she at least wanted answers.

"He was a good, God-fearing man. Much better than I ever was. Good husband, good dad. But that all changed when a Riker County sheriff's deputy decided he wanted to save himself by damning John."

"The deputy planted evidence and John was convicted," Rachel said.

She saw Marcus's hand tighten around the hilt of the knife.

"Never had a chance," he stressed, seething. "Especially after one of his buddies got up on the stand and praised him as an honest, honorable man. They took one look at my brother and decided he wasn't worth listening to. Went to prison in the blink of an eye. And if that wasn't bad enough…" He gritted his teeth.

If Rachel could have, she would have stepped farther away from him. His anger was almost thick enough to feel.

"If that wasn't bad enough, the people who were supposed to protect him while he was forced to be there? They let him be killed in his cell like he was nothing." The anger didn't dissipate. It transformed. From rage to a smile steeped in venom and dripping with violence. "So I decided to wait until I could punish the man who didn't save my brother."

Rachel was almost too afraid to speak.

Almost.

"You didn't just pick the prison transport at random because of opportunity," she realized aloud. "You targeted it specifically."

"After John was killed, Tracy Markinson went through an internal investigation. He was cleared. I knew it was only a matter of time until he was shuffled around. So I waited and waited. And then, *poof.* There he was, tasked with transporting some prisoners. It was like the stars aligned."

Rachel still didn't understand. "Why did you wait? If you were so hell-bent on killing him, why not go to his house? Or get him when he left work one day? *Why kill all those men?*"

Marcus shook his head. He had the gall to *tsk* at her.

"Because no one will hear what you're trying to say if you aren't loud, Ms. Roberts," he said as casually as could be. "And nothing is louder than kidnapping a van full of men and holding them hostage."

Rachel felt sick to her stomach. "You never planned on letting them go, did you?" Her voice was a whisper. "No matter what the sheriff did that day. You just wanted to punish one man. And then, what? Embarrass the department?"

"I wanted them to know what feeling helpless was *really* like," he said simply. "But I couldn't do that if they were all good men, now could I? *That's* why I waited for a transport. I needed someone who was good. Someone they would fight for. Someone like my brother."

Rachel thought she couldn't have felt any worse than she already had. But she was mistaken. Her face turned hot, her hands fisted on reflex, and the only reason she didn't cry was that the rage building within her was too quick. "You needed my husband."

Marcus nodded again. "Tracy was the target, but David was the message. They were both dead before you even knew they'd been taken." He shrugged. "Everything else after that? That was just for show, wasting time while I tried to get my affairs in order. That's when Dane showed up. Luckily, I'd planned ahead. Paid a doctor on standby just in case things—"

"Get out," Rachel interrupted.

It was like she was out of her own body, listening in from somewhere else. Her voice was unrecognizable even to her own ears. Menacing. Angry. Violent. She was seeing red. Blood red.

"Get out," she repeated. Marcus raised his eyebrow. He started to smile. Rachel took a step forward. "Get. Out."

His smile wiped clean. He studied her expression, her body.

"Listen here…" he started. It was his stance that changed now. He hadn't expected her to bite. He'd expected her to sit still and listen. To be the audience to his grand tale. To ask questions he wanted to answer.

He was grossly mistaken.

Rachel took another step closer. Every muscle in her body was coiling. Like a snake ready to strike. Then she was yelling. "Get out! Get out! Get out!"

With adrenaline coursing through her veins, she grabbed the box closest to her, lifted it and swung it around. It was too heavy to reach him, but it still sounded bad as it slammed to the floor in front of him.

"What's going on?" the man behind Marcus asked. His hand was on the butt of his gun. Rachel didn't care. She wasn't going to just stand around and do exactly what the man wanted. She couldn't. Not when he'd just admitted to killing her husband and then playing with their hope just to prove some kind of misguided point.

Not after he'd *used* David's goodness to justify killing him.

No.

She wasn't going to just stand there and take any of the man's madness.

Rachel opened her mouth to repeat her command, but Marcus held up his hand.

"We're going to leave Ms. Roberts alone for a while," he said, already moving out of the shed. "I think she needs some time to cool down."

Rachel felt all the sorrow and pain of David's death washing over her again. This time the rage of knowing his killer and the motive behind it was hot on its heels.

If Marcus stayed any longer, he would meet someone that even Rachel hadn't known existed.

A widow looking to avenge the man she'd sworn to love forever.

Or maybe Marcus did know exactly what was coming and how dangerous it was.

Without another word, look or evil little smile, he shut the door. The sound of scraping filled the shed as he put whatever had blocked the door before in front of it again.

For what felt like forever Rachel stayed in the middle of the shed, hands balled at her sides and rage pulsing through her body.

Then, slowly, it started to drain.

When it was gone, Rachel did the only thing she could.

She cried.

Chapter Nineteen

Tucker Hughes refused to say anything to Dane and Chance. He clammed up so fast that Dane was almost afraid he had passed out. But then he'd looked Dane in the eye.

That was when they both knew that *they both knew*.

Tucker had illegally adopted Marcus Highland's nephew and had been raising him for almost a decade.

The million-dollar question was why.

Dane didn't get to ask it, though. Not before chaos broke out. Not before two men were able to take Rachel straight from the hospital without any pushback. The only silver lining to the situation was that Rachel had managed to once again keep Lonnie out of harm's way the best she could.

Though, instead of pretending like he was okay, this time Lonnie had been shaken. He'd cried as he'd relayed the conversation back to Dane.

"It's my fault," he had said once a search of the

hospital had turned up empty. If Lonnie hadn't been there, Dane would have hopped in his car and joined the motorcade of law enforcement that hit the streets. "I—I should have gone with them the first time. They wouldn't have taken her!"

Dane had been fighting anger at himself and anger at the men who'd taken Rachel. He was fighting fear, too. Worry that they would hurt her—or worse— had nearly overwhelmed him, but he knew that losing focus would only make matters more difficult. He had placed his hands on the boy's shoulders and knelt in front of him.

"Rachel made a choice," he said sternly. "Those men, those *bad* men, wanted to take you. She decided she wasn't going to let them. It was the right choice and one I would have made, too. There was nothing you could have done contrary to that. So stop blaming yourself and let's figure this out."

Lonnie had calmed down enough to get the rest of what the man had said out.

"Marnie is the neighbor," Dane had translated for Chance. "She's Rachel's friend, too. But I don't know who June—" Dane had jumped up like he'd been shocked. "June is Rachel's cat! They're at her house!"

After that Dane had taken Lonnie to the lobby with Suzy and a local police officer. The former had her phone out and was rerouting available deputies to Rachel's house. It was a plan he'd called off once they were in Chance's car.

"Last time we were in a hostage situation with

Marcus Highland and his group, we ended up trying to overwhelm them with our numbers," he had said once she picked up. "I don't want to do that again."

Suzy had trusted his judgment. "Tell us what you want to do and we'll follow you."

It was like a bad case of déjà vu, but Dane had told them what he thought would be the best plan.

Now, less than an hour later, Dane and Chance were at Marnie's house. Her green Beetle was in the driveway, but there was no other sign that anyone else was in the vicinity. Still Dane and Chance searched the house quickly and quietly. But only after they'd broken the front door lock off and let themselves in.

Dane would pay for it later.

"Marcus doesn't leave hostages alive long," Dane said, once they were done. He nodded toward the woods. "This cuts through to the side of Rachel's house. Maybe a three-minute jog. Once we hit the creek it'll be a hundred or so yards after that."

"Are we going to wait for backup to get here?" Chance had his gun out, checking it.

"No," Dane replied on reflex. "At least, I'm not. Wyatt made the decision to try to kill her the other day because she wasn't essential to their goal. They want Lonnie. Not her. I don't want to chance Marcus remembering that, either."

Chance nodded. "I'm not trying to talk you out of it, Dane. We both know how good a shot I am.

I'm all the backup you need." The cowboy flashed a quick grin. Dane returned it.

"Thanks," he had to say. "I mean it."

Chance nodded again. His expression hardened. He looked to the woods. It was go-time.

Dane led the way, wordlessly going into the trees. He had walked the Roberts's property enough with David through the years to be familiar with the land that butted up to it. The woods weren't so dense that they couldn't pass through, but they were thick enough that they could use the surroundings for cover if needed.

Which meant so could the men who had Rachel.

Dane took the direct path between Marnie's house and Rachel's, deciding to cut down on time. He didn't know what the play was anymore. If the goal was to get Lonnie, would they use Rachel as leverage? Or was she bait?

Either way, Dane was done waiting around and asking questions.

A soft buzz in his pocket made Dane pause. He pulled his phone out. It was a text from Suzy. It made his blood run cold. He stopped in his tracks.

"What is it?" Chance asked at his side, voice low.

Dane cussed beneath his breath. "They can't find Lonnie." He said a few more *really* bad words. Chance joined in.

"There's no way they would already be at Rachel's house, then," the cowboy pointed out. "Which means, not only do we have a lead, but—"

"Not all of their men are at the house," Dane finished.

He didn't want to point out there was a good chance they wouldn't go back to Rachel's if they had what they wanted. *Who* they wanted.

"We need to hurry, regardless," Dane said.

"Don't worry, after we get Rachel we'll get Lonnie back, too," Chance assured him.

Dane nodded. He started forward again. "You're damn straight we will."

The two of them hustled until they hit the creek. Dane walked into the water, holding his cell phone and gun above his chest. He didn't think the water was deep enough to go over his head, but it had been a while since he'd swam there. The last thing they needed was to be soaking wet from head to toe and trying to be stealthy.

The water was cold but stayed beneath his ribs. Still not the best conditions for sneaking around, but he wasn't about to waste time trying to find a dry place to cross. Once they were on the other side, Dane kicked off as much excess water as he could and stopped within the cover of a group of trees.

"In a few more yards we'll be able to see the house," he said, nodding in the direction he meant. "It's the side of the house with an elevated deck that leads to a sliding-glass door that opens into the kitchen. If anyone is on that side of the house and looks out, we'll be spotted plain as day once we leave the trees."

Dane tapped the tree trunk with his index finger. "This is the house." He tapped off to the side. "This is us." He traced a half moon above both. "I'm going to use the trees we're in now as cover and run to this tree line that umbrellas the house. From there it's a straight shot to the back door. There's no cover between that tree line and there, but the only windows that have a clear shot of the space between are in the laundry room and a bathroom. Hopefully no one is in either one and looking outside."

"They won't be if I make them look somewhere else," Chance said with a sly smile. He tapped the bark that would be the front yard. "We should disable any vehicles just in case anyone tries to run. I can do that and also look out for anyone who might show up. I can also make some noise to draw their attention. It might be enough to get you in the house without anyone noticing."

"It also puts the spotlight on you," Dane said. "With no backup."

Chance thumped the brim of his hat. "Good thing I'm a great shot." He sobered when Dane didn't laugh. "If Marcus Highland is the one calling the shots and he has Lonnie now, then the window to get Rachel might be closing fast. This is our best plan, boss."

The last time Dane had made a plan, his best friend had been killed. Now there was more on the line. Rachel, Lonnie, Marnie and Chance. The woman he loved, the kid they'd do anything to save, a young woman who meant a lot to Rachel, and a close friend who meant a lot to Dane.

Worry and fear tried to push their way deeper into him. But this time Dane wasn't going to second-guess himself.

"At least it's not storming," he said, pulling his gun up.

Chance nodded. "There is that."

They shared a look that was their version of saying "good luck" and went in opposite directions. Dane followed the trees for a couple hundred yards before they started to thin out. He sprinted to the cover of the next tree line, following it until the back of the house was in view.

No one was in the yard as far as he could see. And even if they had been, a car alarm started going off at the front of the house. Chance.

Dane took a quick breath.

It was now or never.

He held his gun tight and started to run for the back door. The layout of the house in front of him was already pulled up in his mind. Once he stepped through the door, he would be in tight quarters. He'd have to shoot fast if anyone tried to attack. Then he'd have to—

A banging sound pulled Dane's attention to his left. A few feet from the corner of the house was a shed. He'd never seen it before. Rachel must have gotten it recently. It looked brand-new.

Dane switched gears, falling back enough to get a better view of the shed door. Or where the door should have been. A metal container was pushed against it, blocking the bottom half.

And someone was banging on the other side of the door. Even from this distance he saw the force of it shake the structure.

Rachel.

Dane kept his gun high as he ran full-tilt toward the shed. He moved around the side, ready to shoot any guards that might be around, but came up empty. Whoever was in the shed was all-out throwing themselves at the door. Dane holstered his gun and focused on the container. It was an industrial toolbox. One he recognized as David's. The last time Dane had seen it, it had been in the garage collecting dust.

Dane didn't want to call out to whoever was inside for fear it would give away his location. Instead he planted his feet and bent to get a better hold on the toolbox. Even empty, the container was extremely heavy. Definitely a good makeshift lock for a door that opened outward. It took a few grunts and pushes before the toolbox budged, but once he had a good momentum, it was easier to clear the door. Though it scraped something awful against the shed's exterior.

The banging stopped.

Dane pulled out his gun again.

Slowly he opened the door.

"Ahhh!"

Something flew at Dane's head. He dodged to the side, barely missing it. Then Dane was looking at Rachel.

It was like every part of him had been reborn.

Rachel dropped the book in her hand and ran at him. He lowered his gun and pulled her into an embrace he felt in his bones.

"I'm so glad you're okay," he said into her hair. He squeezed once and then pulled away. "*Are* you okay?" Once again her eyes were swollen and red. She'd been crying. He caught one of her hands. Her knuckles were freshly bloodied. No doubt trying to get out.

Rachel nodded.

"Dane, Marcus is alive," she whispered. "He came to talk to me. There was a man with a gun with him. He was also at the hospital with… I'm assuming, Levi. I think Levi and Overalls are in the house, but I haven't seen either of them. Did Lonnie get away?"

Dane nodded but knew his expression had only soured. Rachel tilted her head to the side.

"He was okay, but a few minutes ago I got a message that he had disappeared."

Rachel tensed. "Do you think they're coming back here with him?"

"If Marcus is in the house, I have to imagine so."

Rachel nodded.

"Marnie has to be in there, too. We have to get inside," she said decisively. "We have to end this."

The car alarm stopped.

Dane shook his head. "It's too dangerous. Backup is going to Marnie's." He felt his jaw harden. "I didn't want to repeat what happened last time."

Rachel grabbed his hand.

"Dane, Marcus told me…" She hesitated.

"What?"

Denim-blue eyes bored into his.

"Dane, he said he killed David and the rest of the men before he ever even called the department. There was nothing you or anyone could have done to save them." She squeezed his hand. "They were already gone."

Dane knew he should have felt some small part of relief. His decision to storm Marcus's hideout when his gut told him something was wrong had plagued him for years. He'd gone over that plan thousands of times in painstaking detail. He'd worked through even more what-ifs and any and all plans he could come up with instead. He'd lost sleep, lost confidence, and lost some of his sanity since then. Just trying to understand what had gone wrong. Why he couldn't save his friend.

Now he knew why.

David had already been dead.

That should have made Dane feel some kind of closure, yet all it did was make him mad.

Livid.

Rachel saw it in his eyes.

"This time is different," she said. "This time will end differently."

Dane nodded, feeling the weight of the gun in his hand. "This time—"

Someone cried out behind them. It was a woman. Dane was barely able to keep Rachel behind him as he moved around the corner of the shed to look at the back of the house.

Marcus Highland had walked out the back door and was staring right at them. The only reason Dane didn't shoot him right then and there was the young woman he was holding by the root of her hair.

"Marnie," Rachel yelled out.

She was bloodied but alive.

Marcus smiled and pressed the gun to her temple. "I think it's about time we finally talk face-to-face, Captain."

Chapter Twenty

"Let her go."

Dane's aim was squarely on Marcus while the grinning man's was undeniably on Marnie. Rachel met her friend's gaze. She was in pain. That was clear. Her hands were bound at her side. She couldn't get hold of the hair Marcus was pulling.

"Let her go," Rachel repeated. "Please. You don't need to pull her hair to hold a gun to her head."

It was a crude point to make. It was also accurate. Marcus snorted but opened his hand. Marnie cried out as she fell against the ground. She rolled onto her side but kept quiet.

Rachel's heart squeezed at the sight.

"What's your plan, Marcus?" Dane asked. His voice wasn't chilly. It was downright arctic. "What do you want?"

A gunshot sounded in the distance. Marcus and Dane didn't flinch. Rachel and Marnie did.

"My plan is to finish what I started back then. Back before you ordered me to be shot."

"And what's that? Trying to get the Saviors of the South back into the news? Trying to grab some fame?"

Marcus let out another laugh. It actually shook his stomach.

"The Saviors of the South was a joke," he said. "I wanted vengeance, but I needed help. And some people will do anything for a cause they believe in." He shrugged. "So I made a cause, gave it a name and gave it a voice."

"And then you killed those men and it wasn't enough?"

Marcus's mirth started to wind down. "I didn't expect you to come as soon as you did. It kept me from leaving."

"It kept you from getting Lonnie," Rachel proclaimed.

"I had a backup plan for being shot, for playing dead, for disappearing and living a life, the life my *brother* deserved, but—" He sucked on his teeth for a second. Like he was expressing mild annoyance at the weather or something as mundane as a traffic jam. "But I didn't expect you to come that early. I couldn't grab him. So I got my good, *useless* buddy to take him in. Keep him safe until I could finish what I started. Do right by his father. Make you all pay while showing the rest of the county y'all so-call protect that they're no safer with you than in the prisons you put them in."

"You should have done right by Lonnie," she

snapped back. "You should have raised him, not erased yourself because you'd rather cause more pain than deal with your own."

Marcus didn't like that. He sneered at her. "You're so naive. That's why I wanted you, too. When I realized you were teaching Lonnie, it was like being given a second chance to repeat the past. But to do it *right*. The people might have changed, but our purpose didn't." He looked at Dane. "I can punish the corrupted sheriff's department by killing their captain." His eyes trailed to Rachel. "And we both know which part you'll play."

Anger so bright it nearly blinded her flashed behind Rachel's eyes.

"David," she breathed. "You want to kill me because I'm innocent. Like my husband was. You want to kill me because you can."

"It's poetic, in a way," he confirmed. "They'll feel bad because they couldn't save your husband and then they couldn't save you."

Rachel didn't need to know Dane that well to pick up on the fact that he was reaching a breaking point. Every part of him seemed to be keyed up, ready.

Which was why she placed her hand on his back.

She hoped it calmed him. At least, enough for him to remember there was more to the situation than revenge.

"Then you'll just take Lonnie and leave town?" she ventured. "You'll disappear to someplace far away and raise him? Take him to school? Take him to ball games? Teach him how to drive? You'll be done with vengeance and violence and live a happy, normal life? What about Lonnie? What if he doesn't want that?"

"If you think he'd choose to stay here, you're kidding yourself. Any life with me will be better than the life he has now," Marcus said. He was getting agitated again. "From what I've heard he's already angry at the world. Doesn't have friends. Even the teachers give him grief. He's already a lost cause. I can only make him better."

Rachel had been trying to keep Dane from going off on the man, but she reached her breaking point before she realized what was happening. Dane snagged the back of her shirt with his free hand as she started to run around him, fire in her eyes.

"Did you ever think sticking him with someone who doesn't love him for all these years might have had something to do with his outlook on life?" she roared. "*No!* You just treat all of this like it's some kind of game!"

"Rachel—" Dane complained as she tried to wriggle out of his hold. Marcus's eyes had gone wide like they had in the shed. She wasn't done, though.

"And don't you *ever* call him a lost cause," she yelled. "You don't even know him!"

Rachel was ready to kick it into high gear and destroy the man who had destroyed her family before he could spread his poison to his nephew, but another gunshot from the front of the house exploded. This time it wasn't alone. It sounded like the front lawn had been turned into a war zone.

Marcus and Dane once again stayed their ground. They didn't flinch, but there was definitely some concern. Rachel just hoped whoever was on their side was winning the fight.

And that Lonnie was nowhere near it.

Marcus's expression went blank. When he spoke, it was to Dane.

"You can still save one person," he said. He shook the gun over Marnie's head. "Tell me where Lonnie is and I'll make sure my men don't kill her. One soul is better than none."

Rachel froze. She hoped her face didn't give away her surprise.

If Marcus didn't know where Lonnie was, then who had him?

She glanced at Dane. His expression also gave nothing away. The gunshots ceased in the distance.

"Give me the girl now and I'll tell my men not to kill you," Dane countered.

"You're bluffing," Marcus said. Though a noticeable tremble shook his hand. He was getting antsy.

"I'll tell you what I'm not doing," Dane said. "And that's negotiating. We're past that."

Rachel's breath caught as the world around them seemed to get knocked out of focus.

In hindsight, she'd realize that everyone there knew Marcus was never going to give Marnie up. Just like he'd never planned on letting David live. He was a man who craved violence and wanted to inflict as much pain as possible. There was never any hope that he would do anything differently now than he had done seven years ago.

Yet, when he swung his gun around and pointed it right at her, Rachel was nothing but shocked. Then Marcus pulled the trigger.

Marnie screamed.

Another sound exploded through the yard and echoed through the trees around them.

Rachel waited, for the second time that week, for the pain that came with being shot. But all she felt was something heavy push her to the ground. Then she was staring at Dane's back.

"Dane?" she breathed. It was a whisper. Confused and quiet. "Dane?"

Then the picture around her focused.

Across from them Marcus had dropped to his knees. He was holding his chest with one hand, blood already staining his shirt, and trying to crawl to where his gun had fallen with the other. Rachel looked down at the ground in front of her. Dane was also slow to get to his feet. She didn't understand why until he tried to stand but could only rock backward.

Rachel reached out and caught his back and shoulders against her chest. She looped her hands around him in a one-sided embrace. She looked over his shoulder. That was when she saw the blood at his stomach.

"Oh my God, Dane!"

That was when she realized what had happened. He'd taken a bullet for her.

"Get…get the gun, Rach," he wheezed, pointing. His service weapon was a foot too far away.

If Marcus got to his first, they'd all be dead.

Rachel tried to move out from under Dane, but his muscle mass and injury worked against them. Rachel tried to swallow her rising panic.

"Rach, I—" Dane started. It tore at her how pained the sound was. Her trying to push herself out from under him wasn't helping. Marnie tried to get to her feet to help distract Marcus, but he was already putting his hand around the butt of his gun.

Before Dane could finish his thought and before Marcus could finish them both, another flurry of movement rushed across the yard. However this time it came from behind them.

"Stop!"

Lonnie ran from the tree line and jumped in front of Danc.

"Lonnie!" Rachel pushed herself up against Dane, scrambling to get free. She felt Dane try his best to move. He managed to sit up enough that she slid out.

The boy ignored Rachel and stared at his uncle instead.

"I choose them," he yelled. "*I choose them!*"

Lonnie threw his arms out wide, blocking her and Dane from Marcus's aim. Rachel tore at the grass, trying to get her balance. Her legs didn't seem to want to work. Her adrenaline hampered her speed more than helped.

"Lonnie, run!" she yelled.

But it was like she wasn't there at all.

Marcus kept his gun up and spoke to his nephew.

"You choose them?" Marcus asked, sounding just as surprised as Rachel had been to see Lonnie come out of the woods.

Finally she was able to get up. Her heart was hammering in her chest. She stumbled but managed to jump in front of Lonnie. It was her turn to throw her arms out to block him.

Marcus looked between them.

Rachel braced for his next shot.

It never came.

"You choose them," Marcus repeated. He looked at Lonnie. "Okay."

Marcus Highland dropped his gun.

He died shortly after.

Rachel dove for Dane's gun and turned around, ready to use it without moderation on anyone else who decided they wanted to hurt the people she loved. Thankfully, when the back door flew open a few seconds later, the man in the doorway was wearing a black cowboy hat.

"Chance, Dane's been shot," she yelled, unable to revel in the relief of seeing a friendly face.

Rachel didn't know what Chance did next. She knelt next to Dane and lifted his head to her lap. Lonnie dropped down on the other side of him.

"Oh, Dane!" Unable to keep the tears from rushing out with her words, Rachel issued one concrete command to the man she loved. "You're not allowed to leave me again. You hear me? You're not allowed."

Sirens sounded in the distance.

Dane didn't move.

HOSPITALS.

Rachel had once thought there was nothing worse than being admitted into one. Now she stood corrected. Watching someone you love flat-line in one was the worst. A million times so.

But hearing that same monitor come back to life?

That was a relief unlike any other.

It was that relief that only grew stronger over the next few days. After every surgery and close call passed, with Dane's chance of survival growing.

Now, a week later, staring at the captain from the end of his hospital bed, Rachel felt like she could finally breathe again.

"I'm sure glad you listened to me," she said with a smile. "I didn't like the past few years without you and I wasn't convinced I would like any more without you, either."

Dane snorted. Then cringed.

"Easy, now, Captain," she said. "You got shot in the stomach, you know. Might need to take things easy for a little bit."

Dane slowly waved his hand at her, dismissively.

"It's just a flesh wound," he said, an easy smile gracing his lips despite everything.

Rachel had worried she would never see it again.

"Do you remember talking to me yesterday?" Since the cavalry had come in and taken them to the hospital, Rachel hadn't left his room for more than a few minutes at a time. "You were pretty out of it with the painkillers."

Dane looked thoughtful for a moment.

"Yes and no," he said. "I remember you told me that I was shot, that I was going to be okay even though I'd been shot, and that the man who shot me was dead."

"So basically everything about being shot," she teased.

He snorted and then cringed again. She moved closer to him so she could grab his hand. He squeezed it.

"I also remember that Marcus could have killed you," he said, all humor aside. "And that he could have killed Lonnie, too. The same kid who ran away from Suzy at the hospital, stowed away in Chance's SUV and then followed us. I can't believe he did that."

Rachel nodded. "He told me, and I quote, 'It was my turn to make a decision and I decided to help.'"

Dane hadn't heard that part yet. She didn't miss the small smile that passed over his lips.

"He's a good kid," he concluded. "Even when he's trying to sacrifice himself for us."

Rachel laughed. "I can't argue with that."

Rachel recapped what she already said the day before. The gunshots they had heard were between Chance and three of Marcus's lackeys. He'd slashed their tires and then used the car alarm as bait. Levi had been the first one out. Chance had jumped him, knocked him out and then gone back to hiding. After that Chet, previously known as Overalls, had managed to get a shot off. Chance had been forced to shoot to kill. Then a man named Javier had gone toe-to-toe with the cowboy. Chance had won.

"He's a great shot," Dane said, not at all surprised.

They'd caravanned to the hospital. Marnie had been checked out and only had superficial cuts and bruises. Even though she'd been told to not go to the house alone, she'd forgotten June the Cat's favorite toy. June had already been showing signs of stress at Rachel being gone, so she'd brought the cat over while she'd looked for it—unaware the house had been taken over by Marcus. Now both Marnie and June were fine and at home resting. Though Marnie had spent two nights with Rachel at the hospital, waiting for Dane to wake up.

"How's Lonnie doing?" Dane asked. "Wasn't he with you yesterday?"

Rachel nodded. "For a little bit. He wanted to stay longer, but Billy and he needed to sort some things out." She felt a flutter of excitement in her stomach. She decided to wait until all the bad news was out of the way before she got into the good. "Right now, though, he's actually out with Suzy at the airport."

Dane's eyebrow went sky-high. "Why are they at the airport?"

"Someone had to pick up your dad." Rachel adopted what she hoped was a chiding expression. "Which, by the way…how am I just now hearing about some crazy guy attacking your dad a while back?"

Dane sighed.

"There's a lot we probably should catch each other up on," he said. "It's been a helluva year."

Chapter Twenty-One

Dane saw the cowboy hat before he saw the man.

"Well, if it isn't Sleeping Beauty," Chance greeted. "And here I was starting to get bored."

The man cut him a grin from the love seat against the wall. He motioned to the table next to him and then the side tables. All were covered in flowers. One even had a fruit basket. There had been two cakes, too, but those had mysteriously disappeared after Dane's dad left for the house.

"I didn't bring you any flowers, but I can pop out and grab some weeds I saw coming in that looked pretty good," he continued, grin growing. "You know, the ones that look like daisies."

Dane rolled his eyes and snorted.

"Your presence is always enough, Chance," he mockingly assured him. "Plus, you taking out three armed guys pretty much has you square in my book for life." Dane pointed to the fruit basket. "In fact, why don't you take that?"

Chance changed over to the chair Rachel had frequented the past few days. He shook his head with a laugh.

"We all know how fruit baskets are the worst," the cowboy pointed out. "Especially when there's not chocolate-dipped anything in it. If I wanted to eat healthy, I'd go to the grocery store myself."

The gesture was nice, but Dane agreed. He'd never been a fan of fruit, in his defense, but it had been a pleasant surprise to receive it and, really, all the gifts. News in Riker County traveled at the speed of light. He'd had people stopping by left and right. It had been all Rachel and the nurses could do to curb the attention. While Dane was expected to fully heal, he was still relatively fresh from the trauma of being shot. It still hurt to laugh occasionally and he was a fool if he thought he'd be doing his normal workout routine any time soon.

To prove the point to himself, Dane reached over to grab his water. He felt the soreness stretch and took it slow.

"So, how are you doing?" Chance asked after he was done. There was no denying there was concern there.

"I'm glad this is over," Dane admitted. He stopped what he was about to say and instead confided in his friend. "I feel like I can finally close the book on what happened all those years ago. Honestly, I already thought I had. I thought I'd moved on. But now…now it feels real. Now it feels *done*. Almost like I have a second chance."

"Or a new start," his friend pointed out. "One that I'm assuming involves a certain middle school art teacher. How's she doing, by the way? I haven't had a chance to really sit down and chat since you landed in here."

Dane let out a sigh. He was still tired even after spending half the morning sleeping.

"I've known that woman for years, and let me tell you, she still finds ways to surprise me." Even Dane heard the pride in his voice. "She's in damage control mode, trying to collect everything that fell between the cracks during the case and also deal with the aftermath of it. She has a habit of putting everyone before herself. She even flew in my dad to help out with Lonnie so she could stay near me." Dane snorted. "I think the toughest negotiation of my career was convincing her to go to lunch with Marnie."

"Not that I'm sure you mind having her around," Chance added.

"There definitely are worse things in life." They shared another grin before Dane became serious again. "Once things settle down, I think she'll finally start to process everything. She was really put through the wringer with this one. You should have seen her yelling at Marcus. I swear she would have attacked him with her bare fists if I hadn't grabbed her." Dane started to fist his hand as anger rose in his chest. He took a second to rein it back. "David, Tracy and the other men were dead before the prison van being taken was reported. There was nothing either of us ever could have done to save them. It's still a lot to process. For both of us."

Chance took off his cowboy hat and nodded. He gave Dane a moment to swim back to sturdier emotional ground. "So, part of the reason I haven't been around here is that I've been out trying to tie up loose ends and questions," he started. "I've learned a few things I thought might interest you."

Chance relayed information that Dane had forgotten to look for in all the chaos. He knew the FBI had found the radio equipment with the broadcast, but he hadn't heard anything past that in the bustle of his recovery.

"It was in the upstairs bedroom of a duplex out in Kipsy. There was bubble wrap covering the walls of one of the bedrooms, acting like makeshift soundproofing. Turns out the duplex belonged to Levi's grandparents and was willed to him after they passed. It looks like that's where our motley crew of crazies was meeting until they took up residence at Rachel's."

"Then why soundproof the place if they just planned on moving?"

A disgusted look passed over Chance's expression. "Levi said that's where they planned on taking Lonnie after they grabbed him from the school. They were going to keep him there while they went after you and Rachel. Apparently, Levi and the others told Marcus they were concerned Lonnie might get loud. Marcus didn't want to gag the boy, so he decided to make a room where, no matter how loud Lonnie yelled, no one would hear him." Chance shook his head. "Me and Detective Foster tested it. I yelled my head off and Caleb never heard a thing."

Dane popped his knuckles, trying to get a hold on the new wave of anger pushing through him.

"Which brings me to the dog crates…" Chance continued. His expression lost its edge. His shoulder relaxed a bit. He smirked. "Turns out Wyatt was *really* into crime television shows. On one he saw this group of people confuse the cops by stealing a bunch of random things."

"So he thought he could throw everyone off their trail by stealing two things they needed and then one random thing?"

Chance made a finger gun. "Bingo."

Dane had to laugh at that.

Chance shrugged. "I guess it worked a little," he admitted. "I *did* take the time to go to every vet in the county asking anything and everything about dog crates. But want to know the kicker? I don't think I would have looked into it had they not taken *three* really bizarre things. Two? Maybe. But throw in the dog crates and I couldn't resist diving in."

"I'm sure Levi and Javier regret listening to Wyatt now. They'll be in prison for a very long time."

Chance smiled. "Music to my ears."

Dane knew the topic of Tucker Hughes wasn't far away, so he decided to address it now. "Tucker talked with Lonnie yesterday. I convinced the doctor to let me take a wheelchair in with him. Rachel was there, too. She convinced me that, even though we now know Tucker wasn't anywhere near a saint, he was the only family Lonnie had ever known and Lonnie deserved to ask his own questions."

"How'd that go?"

Dane's heart ached a little. "Lonnie tried playing it tough but did a lot of yelling. Tucker surprised us, though. He actually said all the right things, considering. And not once tried to defend himself. He also offered to answer any of Lonnie's questions about his real parents. He told me where he knew Marcus had kept all the photo albums of them, which I think helped Lonnie." He smiled. The look was genuine. "Then Lonnie did what he does best and surprised us all. He forgave Tucker right then and there."

Tucker might not have loved Lonnie the way he should have, but Dane knew being forgiven by the boy had meant something to him. He'd told Dane right after Lonnie and Rachel had left that if they ever had questions for him about Lonnie or his biological family, they could write him in prison and he'd respond without any ill feelings.

Tucker never said it, but Dane also recognized the relief in the man. The stress of being under Marcus's command since they were teens was finally gone. He was glad everything was over, even if it meant he was going behind bars.

"That kid's something else," Chance said after

a moment passed. "But what happens to him now? Wasn't Marcus his last living relative?"

Dane nodded.

"But just because his biological family is gone doesn't mean he's short on people who care." Dane grinned.

Chance raised his eyebrow, but Dane knew the cowboy caught on to what he wasn't saying.

Then it was Chance who was smiling.

"Well, that boy definitely deserves a happy ending," he said.

Dane couldn't agree more.

RACHEL TOTED A slice of chocolate cake up to Dane's hospital room with a pep in her step and a song in her heart. She'd just gotten good news from Billy and had an even better talk with Lonnie. Now she had cake.

Her good mood only rocketed when she walked into the hospital room and was met with a wide smile from Dane Jones.

"Howdy," he greeted her. "You just missed Chance."

His eyes went to the container. It had a clear plastic top. His eyes widened. "Is that double-chocolate fudge cake?"

Rachel winked. "Good eye, Captain."

She crossed the room, gave him a quick peck and perched next to him on the bed.

"God, you're amazing," he breathed, taking the

cake. "I'm going to save this for tonight, though. That's when my sweet tooth always punches me." He put the container on the side table.

Then he did what Dane Jones did best. He gave her a look that Rachel felt in her bones. It was quiet and perfect and real. It prompted her to finally say what she'd been trying to for days. She took a deep breath and put his hand firmly between both of hers.

Concern crossed his expression. She didn't give him a chance to ask why it was there.

"When you told me you loved me, I didn't say it back," Rachel started. "I should have, but then you gave me that look." She averted her eyes for a moment, searching for the right words. The ones that would make him finally understand.

The ones that would hopefully set him free.

"What look?"

Rachel ran her thumb across the top of his. She met his stare. "That one that said you felt guilty for loving me because of David."

Dane opened his mouth to say something but she cut him off. "Don't try to deny it. I know how you think. How can you be happy with me of all people when David can't be here? *But* I have something to say to that and I want you to listen, okay?"

For a moment she didn't think Dane would agree, but then he nodded.

She took another small breath and then said what was in her heart. "We have a lot of things in common, you and me. But one of my favorite things we share *is* David. You loved him. I loved him. But, Dane, he also *loved* us. Nothing will ever change those facts. Not even if we love each other. And, Dane, I do love you. I really do." She smiled. "And if David knew you were using him as an excuse not to be happy, well, then he'd kick your tail, Dane Jones. And you know that's the God's honest truth."

Dane surprised her with a laugh. Rachel loved the sound.

"You're right," he conceded. "He'd probably go find and put on those boots he got at the rodeo to do it, too. What did he call them again? The really terrible red ones."

"Ass-kickers," she supplied.

Dane chuckled. Rachel kept smiling.

"You see? Just because we can move forward and he can't doesn't mean we've forgotten about him," she continued. "It just means we're moving on. And David would have wanted that for us."

Rachel's eyes widened as Dane pulled his hand from between her own. But then he reached out and grabbed her chin. Gently he pulled her into a kiss.

It was warm and soft and wonderful.

However the most exciting part was everything else that would follow it.

Dane broke the kiss with a smile already across his lips. "One *helluva* year."

Epilogue

"This is madness."

Dane took a step back and ran a hand through his hair. There was no way they were going to be able to pull it off. It was crazy that they were even attempting it.

"I haven't been trained for this," he added.

Rachel rolled her eyes.

"This isn't madness, Dane. This is cake," she deadpanned. "The cake, I might mention, that we had to make and decorate last minute because you *dropped* the last one. Now stop your griping and hand me that bottle of sprinkles."

She might have had her grumpy face on but Rachel's voice let him know she was still amused. Still, he gave her the sprinkles and tried for the umpteenth time to defend his mistake. Or really, shift blame to someone else.

"It's not my fault Olivia decided she wanted to swan-dive off her high chair while I was trying to move it. I made a very valid decision to sacrifice the cake to keep our daughter from busting open her head. I'm sure Cassie will understand."

Rachel dusted the birthday cake with, in his opinion, too many sprinkles. The professional cake they'd bought had been perfect. Their new backup cake? Disaster. But he wasn't going to tell his wife that. Not after she'd been so excited to play hostess for the party.

"I'm not questioning you saving that wild child of ours," she pointed out. "I'm questioning why you moved the cake in the first place when I told you to *not touch it.*"

Dane looked away, trying to act nonchalant.

It made her laugh. "Can you tell me again why you moved it?"

Dane muttered the answer.

"Say again, Captain? I don't think I heard that."

"I was looking for the remote!"

Rachel tried to look stern but it didn't last long. She shook her head and continued to laugh. Dane rolled his eyes and was prepared to launch into another defense when the doorbell rang. Nerves flashed across Rachel's face. He laughed and dipped in to kiss her cheek.

"Everyone is going to love it," he assured her.

She let out a sigh but smiled. "You get that and I'll go get Olivia changed."

Dane complied with the instruction. He didn't stop as Rachel called after him, "And don't move the cake this time!"

It had been a little over three years since the Saviors of the South and their leader had been stopped. In that time a lot had changed and a lot had stayed the same. Dane had asked Rachel to marry him two months into dating and then moved in with her shortly after. He'd been asked if it was weird to live in the family home of her late husband, but Dane had been the one who'd suggested it. David had always wanted to keep the house and the land it sat on in the family, and that was exactly what Dane and Rachel intended to do. David's picture was proudly displayed on their mantel with the rest of their family, and they wouldn't have wanted it any other way.

Dane opened the front door wide and had to adjust his gaze down slightly.

"Hey, Mr. Jones!" Jude Carrington chirped, his red hair wild. He thrust his thumb backward to the car idling in the drive. "Did you see my new ride? Well, I can't technically drive it yet, but my mom said that I can have it when my brother goes to college. Isn't it cool?" Dane gave a wave to Mrs. Carrington and laughed. The car was dated but solid, a dream for a fourteen-year-old obsessed with cars. Which Jude definitely was.

"That's pretty cool," Dane admitted.

Jude nodded again and then yelled into the house, "Hey, Lonnie, come look at my car!"

Dane couldn't help laughing as Lonnie tore out of his room and rushed down the hall toward them like the building was on fire. Dane barely got out of the way as the two jumped off the porch. They were circling the car like sharks in chummed waters when Rachel appeared next to him on the porch. Olivia squealed in delight as Dane stole her from her mama.

"So I guess Patrice finally told Jude he's getting his brother's car when he turns sixteen?" Rachel asked with a laugh. Dane nodded. "He does remember he's not sixteen yet, right?"

Dane shrugged. "Jude rarely lets details like that stop him."

Rachel turned to try to fix the bow in Olivia's hair. It was a battle she lost every time, but that never stopped her from trying.

"Speaking of presents and getting older, are you *sure* we can't give Lonnie one of his birthday presents a little early this year?" She lowered her voice. "I mean, it's only a month away and it's not like he won't get others."

Dane raised his eyebrow. Rachel hurried to sweeten the option. "May I point out that his grades are great and he's been killing it at helping with Olivia? *And*—and this is a *practical* present for a growing artist."

Dane knew when there was a battle that he couldn't win.

"You want to go ahead and buy him the drawing table," he guessed.

Rachel smiled. "It might not be the promise of a car, but to him, it's more. He's been drooling over a

professional drawing table ever since he saw his favorite comic book artist use one."

Olivia grabbed her bow and threw it on the
ground. Rachel picked it up and put it in her pocket.
Dane also lost his fight.

"Fine," he conceded. "You broke me down,
woman."

Rachel winked. "I'm glad you feel that way. Because I already ordered it."

She smirked and tried to run away, but even with a
toddler in his arms, Dane was able to catch her. Both
ladies laughed as he kissed Rachel full on the lips.

"Eww, don't look now, Lonnie," Jude said as they
walked onto the porch. "Your parents are making
out. Let's get out of here!"

Lonnie laughed and followed his best friend into
the house. Rachel looked after them with a smile
clear in her eyes.

Tucker Hughes might have spent his life helping
Marcus plan and commit crimes, but he'd kept his
word to help Lonnie with any questions he might
have. Not only that, he'd even helped Dane and Rachel with their own questions about Lonnie's early
childhood. They would never fully forgive Tucker
like Lonnie had, but there was enough good between
them that they wrote to him and even sent a card or
two. There was no denying that Lonnie had been
shaken by what had happened, but he finally admitted to them that night after they'd talked to Tucker
that he was relieved. He'd spent his short life up

until that point thinking something was wrong with *him* and that was why Tucker hadn't showed him the love he deserved.

If Rachel hadn't already decided to try to adopt Lonnie, Dane was sure she would have right then and there. As it was, the business that the sheriff and Lonnie had to tend to while Dane was in the hospital was Billy setting up temporary guardianship with Rachel. She'd made sure to ask Lonnie first, though, promising him he'd always have a voice when it came to his future. Lonnie had immediately said yes. His adoption had been finalized right after Dane and Rachel were married.

Two days after that he'd asked if he could call them Mom and Dad.

They had also immediately said yes.

Now, for the life of him, Dane couldn't imagine his family without the boy in it.

A car honked, pulling their attention to the driveway. Matt and Maggie Walker parked and got out. Their son Cody had a present in his hands.

"Well, if it isn't the famous true crime novelist," Dane said by way of greeting Maggie. He mussed Cody's hair as Rachel directed him to Lonnie's room. "Does that mean we're famous by association now?"

Maggie waved him off with a smirk.

"One bestseller doesn't make you famous," she said. Matt hooked his arm around her shoulder.

"But that doesn't stop me from bragging to everyone about it." That made his wife laugh.

"He's endearing *and* embarrassing," she said.

"Ah, that should be the official slogan for husbands," Rachel said. She pulled Maggie into the house while Dane and Matt walked around to the side deck. It wasn't long before they were joined by a stream of guests.

Billy and Mara had brought their kids, along with Billy's mother. It was the perfect move, according to Caleb. He and his wife, Alyssa, had a toddler and a baby with them. Apparently he'd thought about asking their friends the Rickmans to come along just so they had an extra helping hand, but Alyssa had worried they would be intruding. Dane laughed that thought off. His dad had spent the first two months in town after Olivia was born helping them stay sane.

"Don't you even dare talking about kid madness," Suzy said, walking out of the kitchen with her own toddler on her hip. Her husband, James, was inside the house with their five-year-old. "We might only have two little ones, but don't let that fool you. We have a teenager and a college graduate."

Billy laughed. "But don't you have that live-in nanny?"

Suzy rolled her eyes but smiled. "If you're talking about Jensen, I wouldn't call him particularly helpful with this one." She motioned to her daughter. "Anytime there's a dirty diaper, he starts gagging. You'd think it wouldn't bother him as much considering he's had a drunk man vomit on him while he was running the bar."

"Oh, are we talking about kid war stories?"

Everyone turned to see Cassie and Henry coming up the stairs. Henry was wearing one of their twins across his chest while holding their toddler son Colby's hand. Cassie had the other twin in her arms. "Because we're late to my own birthday party because this one—" she pointed to Colby "—decided to put a popcorn kernel up his nose. We were two steps from going to the ER before he blew it out himself."

Henry shook his head.

"I'm not too ashamed to say I was more freaked out than she was," he said. "I mean one second it was there and then the next it was gone."

Everyone laughed and the next hour was spent talking, mingling, and swapping old and new stories. It wasn't until after the cake was served and they had all moved out to the seating area around the fire pit in the backyard that Dane felt it.

Really felt it.

Lucky.

Sitting there with the love of his life, the two pieces of his heart, and the closest friends he'd ever had, he just felt plain ol' lucky. He wasn't the only one. Looking across the fire, he caught Billy's eye. The sheriff took off his cowboy hat, smiled and stood. He used the hat to get everyone's attention.

"I know all of us here aren't for speeches, but sitting around and seeing us all has me feeling…well, emotional. And no, before you say anything, it has nothing to do with what I've been drinking."

The group laughed. Billy continued. "It's just that we've all come so far—together—that I can't help saying a few things." His smile grew. Dane leaned in.

"I remember when I started at the sheriff's department," he said. "I was young. I was determined. And I was as stubborn as a mule. I thought Sheriff Rockwell was too uptight, the break room was too depressing, and a certain partner of mine was too cocky." He sent a wink Suzy's way. She snorted. "I thought a lot of things in the beginning, but one thing I never thought was that the department would ever be more than a job. Certainly not become a family."

Billy took a second to look around. Dane didn't need to see their faces to know everyone was in agreement.

"But that's exactly what happened. Through thick and thin—a little too thin sometimes, if you ask me—we've stuck by each other, braved all the storms together, and done it while staying true to what we believe in. This county, the people who live within it, and the good fight for justice. I just wanted to say thank you to all of you for being exactly who you are. And to show how thankful I am, I'm going to embarrass each of you by singling you out." Everyone laughed. Billy turned to Suzy.

"Suzanne Simmons-Callahan," he continued. "When we first started at the department together, you once told me two things. One, don't ever for a second treat you any differently just because you were my best friend. Two, don't ever for a second treat you any differently because you were a woman. I think it's safe to say that none of us here has ever treated you any differently because of either. You have worked hard and true to be one of the best I've ever known in law enforcement all on your own. Nothing and no one has ever stopped you and we've been damn lucky to have you. To Suzy!"

Everyone raised their drinks and cheered. Suzy wiped under her eye. James gave her a big kiss. Billy turned to Caleb next.

Caleb groaned. "Oh boy, this is going to be brutal."

Billy laughed. "Caleb Foster, I remember your first week on the job. You complained more about the heat and humidity than anyone I'd met. It got to the point where I was worried you'd quit just to escape it all."

Caleb nodded. They all remembered that.

"And honestly, I wasn't too keen on you staying in the beginning. But then you proved everyone wrong. You stepped up in the best way possible and never stopped trying to fight the good fight. Once again, I think I speak for all of us when I say how glad we are that you decided to stay and I can't wait to see what you'll continue to do. To Caleb!"

They all raised their glasses and took a drink. Billy homed in on Matt. "Now to our other favorite detective, Matt Walker." Billy took a second to snort. "We've been through a lot. In fact, I think you've been through a lot with everyone here. Sure, it's your job, but I think it's safe to say helping your friends and this county is something you'd do even if you weren't paid to do it. From dropping everything to help those who need it, your time as deputy *and* detective has benefited us all in more ways than we can count. To Matt!"

Matt, closest to Billy, stood and clapped the sheriff on the back. They clinked their bottles together.

"And to the birthday girl and her husband," he continued. "Cassie Ward, we have said from the moment you started at the department that you were the heart of us all. Always a ray of sunshine despite times when work took us into darkness. You never once stopped trying to make us happy, even when it was at your own expense. I don't know where we'd be without you and I don't ever want to find out. To Cassie!"

They all cheered louder this time. Some of the children squealed and cried. Billy ruffled the hair of his son before looking at Henry.

"And then there's this guy." Everyone laughed. "Henry, you're just about the most impressive person I've had the pleasure of working alongside. Stubborn but in a good way. Clever but humble about it. However, I think the most impressive part is how, without a doubt, you're the only person we have ever thought was good enough for Cassie. You make her happy, which makes us happy."

He lowered his voice. "And believe me, we were waiting for her to give us a reason to tear into you."

Henry let out a hoot of laughter. Billy was joking, but was it a joke if it was also true?

"Thanks for being the solid, hardworking guy you are. To Henry!"

Dane raised his glass but skipped taking a drink. Billy's eyes were on him now. Rachel squeezed his hand.

"Dane Jones," he started. He was grinning. "In times of crisis you have told me that I keep this department together, but I just don't think that's true. There was a time in your life when you could have quit, left the department behind, and no one would have blamed you for it. But you didn't. You stayed and kept going, and I don't think you realize how much you've helped us all because of it. Late nights, long weekends, holidays… If there was one thing we could always count on, it was you being there. Even when we didn't realize it. You're the glue, buddy. Always have been, always will be. To Dane!"

Rachel yelled along with the people around him. Dane felt his chest tighten. But in the best way possible. He cleared his throat and stood.

"And now let's talk about the sheriff," he said, grinning at Billy. A second later he sobered. He wanted to make sure his friend saw that he was being sincere. "If Cassie's the heart and I'm the glue, then I don't think I'm being too dramatic when I say that Billy Reed is the soul of not only the department, but Riker County as a whole." A wave of nods spread through the group. "I'd like to think I love this place, but I don't think any of us has a love that compares to yours. You have never hesitated to help any and all of the people who are in our jurisdiction and you've never hesitated to help us, either, for that matter. You take pride in our home and it has showed through every good thing you've done for the department. In turn, you make us proud just to be your friend, never mind your colleague. *We're* the ones who are lucky to have you. Riker County sure is." Dane raised his glass. "To Billy!"

They all cheered. Billy's eyes were glassy, but no one called him on it. Instead they quieted as Billy stood one last time.

"I look around this group tonight, and as I said, I don't see friends or colleagues, I see family," he said. "We've been through a lot and we'll probably be through a lot more. But no matter what lies ahead, I can say without an ounce of hesitation, we will always make it through as long as we have each other. So here's to us and here's to our home." Billy raised his bottle. "To Riker County!"

This time everyone stood.

"To Riker County!"

* * * * *

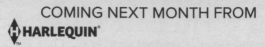

Get 4 FREE REWARDS!

We'll send you 2 FREE Books plus <u>2 FREE Mystery Gifts.</u>

Harlequin® Intrigue books feature heroes and heroines that confront and survive danger while finding themselves irresistibly drawn to one another.

FREE
Value Over
$20

YES! Please send me 2 FREE Harlequin® Intrigue novels and my 2 FREE gifts (gifts are worth about $10 retail). After receiving them, if I don't wish to receive any more books, I can return the shipping statement marked "cancel." If I don't cancel, I will receive 6 brand-new novels every month and be billed just $4.99 each for the regular-print edition or $5.74 each for the larger-print edition in the U.S., or $5.74 each for the regular-print edition or $6.49 each for the larger-print edition in Canada. That's a savings of at least 12% off the cover price! It's quite a bargain! Shipping and handling is just 50¢ per book in the U.S. and 75¢ per book in Canada*. I understand that accepting the 2 free books and gifts places me under no obligation to buy anything. I can always return a shipment and cancel at any time. The free books and gifts are mine to keep no matter what I decide.

Choose one: ☐ **Harlequin® Intrigue**
Regular-Print
(182/382 HDN GMYW)

☐ **Harlequin® Intrigue**
Larger-Print
(199/399 HDN GMYW)

Name (please print)

Address   Apt. #

City   State/Province   Zip/Postal Code

Mail to the Reader Service:
IN U.S.A.: P.O. Box 1341, Buffalo, NY 14240-8531
IN CANADA: P.O. Box 603, Fort Erie, Ontario L2A 5X3

Want to try two free books from another series? Call 1-800-873-8635 or visit www.ReaderService.com.

HI18

SPECIAL EXCERPT FROM

HHARLEQUIN®

I N T R I G U E

*Author Tessa Jane Clementine, known by her readers
as TJ St. Clair, is receiving threatening letters from
a man claiming to be her biggest fan. Silas Walker, a
handsome loner, is the only person who can protect her,
but can she trust him?*

Read on for a sneak preview of
Rogue Gunslinger
by New York Times *bestselling author B.J. Daniels.*

Chapter One

The old antique Royal typewriter clacked with each angry stroke
of the keys. Shaking fingers pounded out livid words onto the old
discolored paper. As the fury built, the fingers moved faster and
faster until the keys all tangled together in a metal knot that lay
suspended over the paper.

With a curse of frustration, the metal arms were tugged apart
and the sound of the typewriter resumed in the small room. Angry
words burst across the page, some letters darker than others as the
keystrokes hit like a hammer. Other letters appeared lighter, some
dropping down a half line as the fingers slipped from the worn keys.
A bell sounded at the end of each line as the carriage was returned
with a clang, until the paper was ripped from the typewriter.

Read in a cold, dark rage, the paper was folded hurriedly, the
edges uneven, and stuffed into the envelope already addressed in
the black typewritten letters:

Author TJ St. Clair
Whitehorse, Montana

The stamp slapped on, the envelope sealed, the fingers still
shaking with expectation for when the novelist opened it. The

fan rose and smiled. Wouldn't Ms. St. Clair, aka Tessa Jane Clementine, love this one.

***

TJ St. Clair hated conference calls. Especially this conference call.

"I know it's tough with your book coming out before Christmas," said Rachel the marketing coordinator, her voice sounding hollow on speakerphone in TJ's small New York City apartment.

"But I don't have to tell you how important it is to do as much promo as you can this week to get those sales where you want them," Sherry from Publicity and Events added.

TJ held her head and said nothing for a moment. "I'm going home for the holidays to be with my sisters, who I haven't seen in months." She started to say she knew how important promoting her book was, but in truth she often questioned if a lot of the events really made that much difference—let alone all the social media. If readers spent as much time as TJ had to on social media, she questioned how they could have time to read books.

"It's the threatening letters you've been getting, isn't it?" her agent Clara said.

She glanced toward the window, hating to admit that the letters had more than spooked her. "That is definitely part of it. They have been getting more…detailed and more threatening."

"I'm so sorry, TJ," Clara said and everyone added in words of sympathy.

"You've spoken to the police?" her editor, Dan French, asked.

"There is nothing they can do until…until the fan acts on the threats. That's another reason I want to go to Montana."

For a few beats there was silence. "All right. I can speak to Marketing," Dan said. "We'll do what we can from this end."

Don't miss
Rogue Gunslinger by B.J. Daniels,
available October 2018 wherever
Harlequin® Intrigue books and ebooks are sold.

www.Harlequin.com

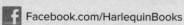
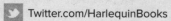